Making of a Lawman

Plainsman Series
Book 2

Simon Fairfax

Corinium Associates Ltd

Making of a Lawman

Published by Corinium Associates Ltd.

A CIP catalogue of this book is available from the British Library

ISBN: 978-1-7391470-5-1

Info@simonfairfax.com

www.simonfairfax.com

Also by Simon Fairfax

Also by Simon Fairfax

The Deal Series

A Deadly Deal

A Deal too far

A Deal with the Devil

A Deal on ice

A Knight and a Spy -road to Agincourt Series

A Knight and a Spy 1410

A Knight and a Spy 1411

A Knight and a Spy 1412

A Knight and a Spy 1413

A Knight and a Spy 1414

A Knight and a Spy 1415

The Plainsman Series

Law of the Gun

Making of a Lawman

Chapter One

The dust hung in the air, creating red clouds of throat-clogging dirt. Everyone was streaked with sweat and raw with tiredness and hunger. It had been a long drive.

The air was filled with bellows from the cattle and shouts from the men as they completed the last full day of the drive. Cowhands whooped and hollered at the errant beasts, herding them as they tried to break free to graze the lush grass off to the sides of the trail that had been forged by many cloven hooves before them.

The sun was getting low in the sky and the glow of the campfire was becoming more evident by the side of a narrow river as light faded with the onset of dusk. It made the men who were herding the cows even more determined to get them up to the river, give them their head and get them across before the light disappeared. Once crossed and watered, they knew the cows would settle, happy with fresh grass and tired after a day on the trail, with water in their bellies and cud to chew. The drag was now being supported by others who had led the herd, reinforcing the swarm of movement, urging the cattle across the river to join their mates. The last action of the day was frenetic, brought on by the tiredness that came from weeks in the saddle. Tempers were fraught as they fought rough weather, drought, herd cutters and Indians on their drive up through the Nations from Texas.

Off to one side of the action sat the man who had been the trail boss for the drive. He looked as creased and worn down as the men who had followed him over the many miles of hardship. His youthful looks belied the mantle of authority that he carried. He reached up to remove his Stetson, wiped his forearm across his sweated brow, then ran his fingers through his blond hair with his other hand. They came away wet and dirty.

"Damn, I need a bath," Nate Carlton muttered to himself, his voice cultured and not at all western in its accent. The big buckskin horse he sat upon nodded its head against the flies that came back after each shake of its handsome head, apparently agreeing with its rider. "I know, old horse, I know. Soon we'll have you in a cool stable with a full bag of oats." Nate patted the horse's neck. He replaced his Stetson and squinted against the low sun, seeing a rider canter up from the riverside.

Jas Box rode with the easy slouch of a westerner born to the saddle. He was part Indian and had been an army scout in the war. Now he worked for one of the small spreads in the Nations and had joined up with the collection of smaller ranches and steadings on the previous drive the year before. His coal black hair flowed in the wind as he pulled his horse to a stop by Nate's side.

"Well, Nate, they're all there and settled and tomorrow we'll see Dodge again. You did it! You brought a thousand head up from Texas, pickin' up more along the way. I count over two thousand head going to market tomorrow. You are a trail boss, sir, and no mistake," Jas said, complimenting the lean young man at his side.

"I swear you'll have me blushing." Nate shrugged off the compliment. "If we hadn't met because of a few stray cows and an attempt to hang poor old Jim, I'd never have known you or any of the others, and I'm sure I'd never have had the idea to form a herd made up of small spreads."

"It sure as hell worked tho', didn't it? You bossed her all the way, got us through everything. You'll have spreads flocking to you now, wanting you to take a herd every year. They'll all want to be part of the Carlton Herd Drive. You've built a reputation, that's how it works out here. A man lives or dies by his reputation, an' you're sure buildin' yours. Credit to you, man."

"Well, I can't say that I'm not proud of all we've done, and I learned a whole lot more along the way. We're also showing how the South can get back on its feet financially and make it work again. Lot of bad things happened in the war, and we've got to make 'em right. But I will say this. It's not a sight I'll ever get tired of, seeing a trail herd on the move, crossing so many miles of country and coming into Dodge at the end of a drive. All adds up to a man being satisfied. But I certainly could use a bath and a change of clothes."

"Yes, sir. I don't know who smells worse downwind, us'n or the cows," Jas joked.

"Might even take a cold bath before supper in that river."

"Well, they put a screen up for Mary Lou and Sue, and if they done 'n' finished, I reckon you won't be alone."

Nate nodded in agreement. Mary Lou's father had been against her coming on a second drive after her friend had been shot by herd cutters the year before, but she was adamant and wanted to lay flowers on Rusty's grave. She was a strong-willed young woman from one of the local spreads, and she was the drive's cook, having traveled down to Texas from her home in the Nations. With Sue, another young Texas rancher's daughter, she had cooked and managed the chuck wagon and bedroll wagon for the drive. The pair had driven the wagons with skill and kept everyone fed with no complaints. They took no nonsense from the men.

Nate and Jas loped off towards the herd, heading for the chuck wagon where Mary Lou stood by the fire doling out hot stew and biscuits. Her dark curls were all fluffed out from washing, her blue eyes clear now of all the dirt and dust. She had matured into a very pretty young woman, Nate noticed. She'd carried a candle for Nate on the last drive, but she had realized with the maturity of her sex that it was not to be. She now sported a pistol at her hip and the girls wore practical divided pants, cowboy boots and men's shirtwaisters, and Stetsons hung from storm straps at their throats. The cook's louse, Sue, had worked as hard as any man, and flashed Nate a smile as he approached.

"And the trail boss comes in last as usual," she commented.

"That's me, ma'am. First to start, last to finish." He offered her the old response.

"Shame you didn't take time to bathe before you ate," Mary Lou chided him. "Wasn't sure if that was a skunk comin' into camp or a dead coyote."

Nate grabbed his plate before responding, knowing it would be forfeit after his response, speaking between mouthfuls as he wolfed down the food, his hunger brought on by a long day in the saddle. With a twinkle in his eye he responded, "Thing is, Mary Lou, some of us have to work on this trip, not just laze around all day in the sun."

Her response was un-ladylike, and with the threat of never cooking a meal again for a worthless trail boss her language was not that of a well brought up rancher's daughter.

Nate held up the hand that wasn't holding his plate in mock surrender and with his meal finished, he headed for the river to bathe.

It had been a tough drive, he thought, as he wandered towards the bank, dimly lit by the campfire. The sun flashed scarlet streaks across the twilight in a spectacular Kansas sunset, with the promise of a clear sunny day to follow. *I've come a long way*, he mused to himself as he undressed, exchanging a few words with other hands that were dressing themselves in the cooler evening air and shivering from the cold water. He wondered where he would go and what he would do now. The trail season was over with the end of the summer, and he could maybe drift west and see some new country. *But where to go and what to do now? Trail season's over, maybe drift west and see some new country.*

His thoughts turned to a pretty auburn-haired girl that he had met briefly on a riverboat near Charlottesville. A cloud came over him as he thought of Sam Kennedy, killed by Brian Wallace after Nate had killed his brother. Nate's actions against Chord Wallace had resulted in a second gunfight with Brian at the DR Connected what seemed like a lifetime ago. The girl had given him an open invitation to call on her if he was ever in Langtonville, despite her stuffy, overbearing mother.

The next day, having settled the herd into the holding pens at Dodge, those same thoughts were with him as he strolled along Front Street, pleased to be back in a bustling and vibrant town after months of desolation and emptiness. He had never quite been able to reconcile his pleasure in comfort and the good things in life with the beauty and wide open spaces of the prairie and mountains. He went into the Long-horn saloon, pushing open the doors, and was assailed by the smell of cooked food, good whisky, tobacco smoke and beer. Nate paused at the doorway, stepping to one side, remembering Sam's words and allowing his eyes to adjust to the dimmer light. Satisfied, he moved across the room to the dining area.

He had agreed to meet with Paul Tranter, cattle buyer, financier and Nate's business partner. He saw him settled over lunch, in the process of finishing a steak and green beans, a glass of wine by his hand. He looked well, and as spry as ever, Nate thought. The half-moon spectacles were perched upon his nose as he read a newspaper, his longish grey hair swept back from his face. He wore his customary fancy silk vest, and a well cut suit covered his lean frame. He looked up as the talk swirled with Nate's entry. The herd had been one of the first to come in this season and with it came a feeling of prosperity to the town that was much valued by its citizens.

Paul Tranter's face broke into a broad smile. "Nate, you old devil! I heard that you were due in today. I was just finishing my lunch and I was going down to the stockyards to see you. Come, sit and tell me all. Let me order you a steak and a glass of wine, I'm bound you'll be needing it. Or something stronger, maybe?"

Paul's welcoming manner soothed Nate better than any salve. He liked the man immensely and always felt that with his astute mind, there would always be a solution to every problem. He reminded him in many ways of his dead father and thought him no worse for that resemblance.

"No thanks, wine will do me well. A steak, some green beans and potato au gratin."

A waitress came over and Paul ordered for him.

"So did you have any trouble?"

Between sips of the Burgundy, Nate responded. "More than our fair share. Indians, then a group of herd cutters tried the state head tax again. We got lucky. One of them recognized me from somewhere, called out my name to the leader and they just rode off." Nate shrugged unsure why.

"Your reputation is spreading, and not just with cattle. Troublemakers will give you a wide berth. The story of you breaking Brannigan's bunch has become the stuff of legend."

"Well, I wish it wouldn't," Nate stated emphatically, then changed the subject, not wishing to be considered a gunfighter. "We brought in close on two thousand five hundred head. Here's the tally book with all the details." Nate reached inside his jacket and produced a scuffed and dog-eared notebook that he laid on the table.

Tranter adjusted his spectacles, and looked at the numbers allocated to those who had supplied the beef. "Three hundred of your own stock, too, Nate. You're building, man, you're building. You'll be a cattle baron soon." He smiled over the top of his spectacles at him.

"I bought a small spread down in Texas. It's not much but I use it as a base. I can hold some young stock there. The land was dirt cheap, and I've settled a file of claim against it, so it's all mine. You remember Billy Jo from last year?" Tranter nodded, intrigued at how much Nate had achieved through his foresight. "Well, I left him down there with another man to mind it while I'm away. It's a start, and I'm building a good base for a herd. My father always spoke of bringing in some Herefords to cross breed with longhorns. Add some more meat and flavor, so he said. Seems like a good idea and I might explore it further and get some shipped from England. I'll try and get in touch with my brother if he's not serving abroad with his regiment."

"Did you hear anything after you notified him of your parents' deaths?"

"Nope. Not a word. I hope he's alive. He's probably off somewhere fighting for queen and country."

Nate's food arrived and he tucked in like a starving man.

He was halfway through his meal, discussing matters with Tranter between mouthfuls, when the door to the saloon burst open and a voice called out to him. Saloons didn't often play host to young, respectable women, and the working girls there turned their heads to look at the newcomer, shooting daggers with their eyes.

"Nate, you better come quick. We got trouble at the stockyard!" Mary Lou shouted across the silence.

"What is it, Mary Lou?" Nate asked as he turned and rose, placing his hat upon his head as he went to her.

"There's a man down at the stockyard claims that we double branded his stock with a straight iron and that you rustled his cattle and wants to talk to the trail boss and no one else. Got his gun ready and says he'll shoot anyone who tries to stop him."

"Alright, I'll be right there. Don't fret now." Then he did something that was now a reflex action, taught to him by Sam. He bent and tied the pigging thong trailing from the tip of his holster to his leg. That done, he settled his gun belt to his satisfaction and walked from the saloon with Mary Lou. "You go and fetch Sheriff Bassett," he told her. "I don't want trouble if I can help it." The girl shot him a questioning glance, looking down at his gun belt. "Go on, now, shoo," Nate urged, and Mary Lou scurried up the street toward the sheriff's office.

In the manner of western towns, those who had overheard the exchange between Nate and Mary Lou began muttering, and men made to leave and follow Nate. They all wanted to see what would happen at the stockyards.

Nate heard footsteps behind and saw that Paul Tranter had risen, placed his Planter's hat upon his head and was coming to back him up.

"They're my cattle, too," he said, a grim expression upon his face.

Chapter Two

The stockyards lay to the west of the town at the end of Front Street, a few hundred yards away. Nate strode toward them, wondering what he would find at the yards and how this trouble could have been caused. He was puzzled at how a man could come all the way up from Texas or even the Nations and claim that his cattle had been mixed up with theirs and that they had been re-branded with a running iron. Something in his mind didn't sit right. He began looking at it like a chess game, trying to see what angles could be exploited and who stood to gain from it.

"Watch my back if you would, Paul. Something here seems off and I don't know what it is."

"Sure. It might be a setup with someone trying to cut a rusty. Let's see how the land lies."

As they walked, the sound and smell of cattle became stronger, and the sweet smell of cow and manure permeated the air. The stores petered out and the tented homes of newcomers became more prevalent as Dodge had started to grow. What was odd was the lack of human sound— it seemed like an almost palpable tension was in the air.

Coming to the corner of the tented city, Nate left the main street warily, looking up at the buildings to the rear of the commercial property with pitched roofs. Sharpshooters in the war had used them to ambush unsuspecting Reb forces coming into a seemingly deserted town. It had been a massacre and he had barely escaped with his life.

Seeing the ring of men by the cattle chute, Nate unconsciously slipped the thong off his Navy Colt. A little behind him and to the rear, Paul Tranter raised the Henry he was carrying to the port arms position. The crowd behind was cautious, but the whisky and beer talking was making its own noise.

The semi-circle of Nate's own trail crew turned and parted like the Red Sea, and through the opening Nate saw three men, the leader to the fore, the others flanking him, both holding Henry repeater rifles, barrels pointing at his own crew. All three were expectant, strung out and ready for trouble.

They look nothing like farmers or ranchers to me, Nate mused.

The leader he saw was fresh-faced, probably no more than a year or two older than Nate. He wore range clothes, but they were too fancy for cow herding. He was a dandy with a two-tone calfskin vest buttoned down the center. A gun belt sat around his waist, tied down, with the well-worn grips of an Army Colt showing above the holster and tiny marks on the wood of the walnut. The thong was off and the man was primed and ready. His whole being shouted violence to Nate's eyes. This was not a farmer seeking compensation, it was a setup, and the men were loaded for bear.

Nate carried on walking through the gap, surreptitiously scanning the buildings about him. He couldn't see anyone who looked suspicious, but that didn't mean that they weren't there. Nate wanted the advantage of the long guns nullified, and the closer he came to the leader and the two flankers, the better that was. He moved diagonally, slightly to the right of the leader.

"You, mister. You the trail boss I've been hearin' 'bout?" the dandy asked.

Nate said not a word and kept getting closer.

"Hey, I'm talkin' to you."

Nate was now only fifteen feet away and close to the flanker with the rifle. He would have to move first, bringing the long barrel to bear. Nate stopped. "That would be me. How may I help you? I understand that there may be a problem with the branding. Be happy to sort it out if I can," he finished conversationally.

A wolfish grin spread across the gunman's face—for that is what he was, Nate saw, a gun hand out to make a reputation for himself. The next words proved it.

"Are you Nate Carlton?"

"That I am, and like I say, I'd be pleased to help you," Nate said gently, playing for time. He wanted the sheriff to arrive now, but there was no sign of him. If he could just get this done without gunplay, it would be better for all concerned. But those who were familiar with Nate sensed that the passive attitude did not ring true with the man they knew. Some of them had seen him in action against Brannigan the year before, and it was always the calm before the storm.

Then Nate did an odd thing. He turned to his left, looking over his shoulder and addressing Mary Lou's father said, "Jim, how about you and a couple of boys bring up some steers and we can look at these disputed brands with mister... Say, what was your name?" It was all said in a conversational manner, but as Nate turned back to the trio his right hand was holding a cocked Colt Police Special from the cross draw holster. No one had seen him draw. But there it was, ready to go. Tranter had followed and now his rifle pointed at the right hand flanker.

"Now, mister, this conversation is over, and tell the fool next to you that if he twitches again with that Henry, I'll spread your belly all over the ground and I'll still get him before you die."

The young gunman's face was furious. He thought that he had Nate boxed in, and now the tables had suddenly been turned.

"Now drop the rifles and you, whatever your name is, drop the gun belt—now!"

Rage suffused the face of the gunman. He'd set a trap and now he had forfeited the advantage. Sweat beaded upon his forehead as the open barrel of the snub nosed revolver loomed large before him . At this range he knew that Nate would not miss. Just one twitch and the hammer would fall, sending a bullet smashing into him. Time stood still. It had seemed so perfect in his mind. Set his man up, go for a showdown and be known from that point on as the man who had outdrawn and killed Nate Carlton. But that gun had appeared so fast, the draw completed in the blink of an eye, and for the first time self-doubt was setting in— was he that fast? Tension wracked his body. He was desperate to make a move but knew it would result in his death. Then it was taken out of his hands.

Others of Nate's crew, not gunmen but loyal to their brand, had pulled their six guns and looked competent, ready to take a hand and reinforce the will of their leader. The crowd behind fell silent, taking in what they had seen. Nate Carlton, trail boss and gunman, had done it again: faced down three men and taken them without a shot being fired. It would be the stuff of legend the minute they returned to the saloon to drink his health. Then a figure pushed through the crowd. It was Sheriff Bassett, with a deputy at his side, closely followed by Mary Lou.

"What the hell's goin' on here?" he shouted, then saw the man Nate was pointing his gun at. "Wes Palmer. I might have knowed it. You tired of livin', boy?"

"Didn't do nothin', Sheriff. Just wanted justice for some cows I figured were mine. Then this gunny here drew on me and my pards," Palmer whined, hurt innocence in every word.

Bassett snorted in disgust, motioning with his drawn Colt. "Get over here, but drop that belt first," he ordered.

Palmer complied, letting the belt slip to the ground as the other men flanking him put their rifles upon the ground next to it and held their hands in the air away from their gun belts. The deputy retrieved the guns and marched all three of them off. As they passed, Charlie Bassett said: "Obliged to

15

you, Nate, for not shooting these buzzards out of hand. Woulda cost the town three funerals." He laughed sardonically.

Nate nodded with a tight lipped smile, letting the tension ease from his body as he pinwheeled the Colt before flipping it back into the holster at his waist.

"My pleasure, Sheriff. Anything to avoid trouble." He tipped his hat and turned to the trail crew. "OK, boys, show's over. Let's get these cattle sorted for shipping."

The crowd came back to life in a mutter of conversation, returning as a mob to the saloon to drink, exaggerate and talk over all they had seen.

"That took restraint and a lot of courage, Nate," Tranter said. "I'm proud of you. You could have charged in there blasting away, and no doubt you'd have got the job done. Mighty fine work."

"I don't know, Paul. Sometimes I think that I'm too eager to settle it with a bullet. I wanted to prove to myself that I could do it without another killing."

Tranter raised an eyebrow. "Just make sure that your morals don't get you killed. They say that Palmer's as fast as a mean rattler. You did well, and no mistake. Now let's go and finish that wine."

The rest of the day passed without incident, and in the time honored tradition the trail crew headed to the saloon to drink and celebrate the end of the drive. The saloon was alive with the rinky-tink of the piano, and the painted dance hall girls plied their trade, made up and dressed in outfits that would not be allowed upon the street in daylight hours.

Because of the girls present on the drive, and in honor of

Rusty, who died on the trail the year before, the men—many of whom had families back home and were not typical young cowhands—had agreed to organize a barn dance with some of the locals and their wives. It was as much a celebration of the herd coming in as the cowhands toasting their success. The town had grown, and more families, storekeepers and others who made up the community, had moved to live there. The barn dance meant that the two girls on the chuck wagon could come along and dance, too. It kept the youngsters less rowdy and the older family men happy.

Nate had never been a big drinker, apart perhaps from wine with a meal, which was a luxury he treasured. His father had taught him to appreciate the finer things in life, of which wine was one, and he loved to sample a good vintage when he could. He now stood at the side of the barn dance, puffing gently on a cigar with a glass of wine in his hand, chatting to Mary Lou after admiring the dresses he had bought for her and Sue as a thank you for all their work.

"Why, you're a southern gen'leman, sir, I do declare," she said, exaggerating a southern drawl for his benefit with a twinkle in her eyes.

Nate smiled in response. After last year, Nate knew that she would not take it to heart. As pretty as she was, he could not settle with her in a tiny part of the Nations. He needed to see more country and spread his wings. He also thought of other women he had met along the way. Settle down? No, he was far from ready for it.

"Well, ma'am," he began as the band started to break into the opening bars of a waltz. "Will you do me the honor of this dance?" She took his arm, and they sailed gaily across the floor, spinning and floating around with the others who were enjoying themselves.

It was hours later that Nate took leave of the party, having decided that he had had enough and needed to sleep. The younger set were still in full flow, and many of them were so drunk that their dancing was shambolic. But it was a good-natured affair, and everyone seemed to be having a grand time. Nate tipped his hat to Mary Lou and slipped out into the cool night air, puffing on his final cigar of the evening, allowing the smoke to dribble out of his mouth into the dark night, enjoying the fragrant tobacco.

The dance hall was situated to the east of the town, just beyond the limits of the houses. Nate wandered easily back into the more densely populated street of buildings. Noise came from one end of the street where the saloons were, but here it was quieter, just the nighttime chorus of the cicadas and the odd snuffle or clip of a hoof as horses waited patiently for their riders. Little stirred, but in the silence Nate heard a click. It was a familiar sound, and the hairs upon his neck stood up. The old feeling of being watched returned, the one brought on by the war and by riding dangerous trails. His feet hit the raised sidewalk as he went up, and he stopped by a post supporting the veranda above, making to steady himself as if unsteady with drink. He put an arm out, puffed once more on the cigar causing it to glow and placed it in the vee of one of the two slanting supports that stopped at about head height. He wedged his hat into the other side, then dropped down quickly, rolling onto the sidewalk away from the post. He started to feel a little foolish, telling himself he was jumping at shadows, yet as he did so the whine of a shot rang out, passing where he had stood a second before. A heavy slug thudded into the thick pine walls behind where he had been standing.

Nate rolled again as another shot trailed him, ending up behind a horse trough. A second flash from across the street betrayed the presence of another long gun that spat from a different direction. He pulled the Colt Police Special from his shoulder holster. It was all he had worn to the dance, leaving behind his long barreled Navy. Against a rifle he may as well have a knife, he knew. He looked to his left, seeing the welcoming corner of the store front only feet away. Another two shots rang out, one hitting the thick trough, the other whining away in a ricochet, at which Nate called out in apparent pain: "Agh! You got me, don't shoot. I'm done for, bleeding to death."

A ribald laugh, manic in its tone, came from the other side of the street. "Whatcha gonna do now, mister big tough gunfighter?" a voice called out.

Nate had banked on someone checking to see what all the shooting was about, but then he guessed that everyone would think it was just high spirits from the roundup crew letting off steam. Another shot came over the trough, sending splinters flying from the back wall behind. Nate knew he had to move. He holstered the Colt, pulled up his knees, rolled onto his front and with a pull of his arms he jackknifed forward to hit the edge of the sidewalk, rolling away into the inky black shelter of a side alley.

Two shots followed him, as the gunmen were caught unawares at the sudden movement. They had thought him too injured to move, especially with such speed. Now, shielded from view in the alley, Nate rose, drawing his gun once more.

"Now we'll see how you like it dished out," he muttered. To go back toward the outskirts of the town would be foolish, he knew. If they had horses there, they'd be long gone and it would expose him to shots. So he moved left, deeper into the town. Reaching a crossroads, he crossed at the shortest point, running low and fast, expecting a slug to hit him at any time. None came.

They're on the run, he thought. Moving left into the shadows he stopped, listening for any sound. Hearing the scuff of boots on dirt, he identified the direction and moved cautiously into the back alley from where the sound had come. Picking up a stone, he threw it against the wall, but no shots came. Then he heard the sound of leather on wood, little more than a whisper in the dark. Were they going up to a room? Nate switched back along the alley and came out onto the street, and sure enough it was a boarding house that stood before him. Whoever had laid for him was bedding down there. The glow of light showed in the window from an oil lamp, and he saw movement as the drapes were drawn. He rapped gently upon the windowpane of the door, startling the landlady who was locking everything up for the night. He persuaded her to open for him and described Wes Palmer.

"Sounds like him. He registered today with another two fellas. My rooms board two, so he an' the dark haired man are sharin'. Rooms at the top of the stairs at the end of the corridor. Mister, I mind who you are and I don't want no trouble."

"Neither do I, ma'am, and I didn't ask those two fellas to lay for me, but they did and my life isn't worth a dime until I get them off my back. Now, would you allow me to arrest them while you fetch the sheriff? He'll possibly be dozing at his desk, but he'll come running to help, of that I'm sure."

The landlady looked at him, then nodded. "Well, I guess killin' trail bosses is bad for business, so I'll do it. But try not to kill anyone."

She pulled her shawl around her, sniffed and left him to face the darkened hall and stairs before him. He moved as quietly as he could towards the staircase and edged up the boards to the landing. Two steps at the top creaked, sounding like the crack of a bullwhip. Nate cursed, waiting for a door to be flung open and shots to be fired at him. Instead, he heard a sash window being raised, wood squeaking against the frame. He turned and ran down the stairs as quietly as he could, playing a hunch and running out through the door to the back alley he had just vacated.

As he lurched around the corner he saw two figures silhouetted darker against the night sky in the ambient light of an oil lamp above. He could not bring himself to shoot them in cold blood, so he called out, flattening himself against the wall to make himself a smaller target that was harder to discern. "Hold it or I shoot!" he called out into the night.

The two figures halted, dropping the boots that they carried. The men turned fast, bringing the rifles in their right hands to bear, their left hands moving to grab the barrel. They needed to cock and work the loading lever.

Nate didn't hesitate. At this range the Henry would have

21

an advantage if it could be brought to bear. He dropped to a crouch, firing as fast as he could, slipping the hammer on the recoil, one for the first man and one for the second. He kept firing until his gun was empty. Six shots echoed through the dark night, amplified by the alley walls, and there was a sodden thud of a bullet against flesh and the cries of the men he hit. Nate knew that the gun fired high, and he had aimed at the center mass. He dared not do anything else when faced with two deadly opponents bearing rifles. He ran forward, wanting to close the distance as he was out of bullets and the Police Colt was now useless except as a club. One of the men on the ground moaned in pain. The other was clearly dead as the final bullet, going high, had ripped out his throat.

Nate looked down at the scene before him, shaking his head. Two more dead at his hand, yet he had gone out of his way to avoid it. He heard footsteps and the sound of voices raised in alarm. In the distance, the glow of lamps and torches moved toward him.

Best go and get my hat, he thought.

Chapter Three

Nate headed out of town the day after the shooting, heading east, claiming he was going to board a train and see New York. Instead, once clear, he circled around, losing his tracks in the cattle trails, and headed west. The only man who knew his true destination was Paul Tranter, who had been sad to see him go but understood his feelings and reasons.

He had not wanted a showdown with some other trigger-happy gunny, hunting a reputation as the man who killed Nate Carlton. He wanted his growing reputation to die off in the east while things cooled down. The sheriff had been fair, partly blaming himself for releasing the three men despite confiscating their pistols until they left town. It had not been enough, yet Bassett had declared it a fair shooting and told Nate he was free to go.

Nate's spirits were raised by the idea of seeing some new country and maybe the thought of speaking again with Isobel Hart - as long as her mother would let her see him. "We'll see, horses, we'll see if I can find Langtonville without getting myself shot at," he muttered as he loped along, trailing Buck as he rode Patch, the large Appaloosa quarter horse stallion he had rescued from his parents' home before burning it to the ground. He moved on at a good pace, bypassing Scout City and making for Cheyenne Wells.

The town was a small stopping off point for the stagecoach from Kansas City to Denver, Nate learned, and the wells from which it gained its name were located south of the junction of the Smokey Hill River where the town straddled the waterway. Nate saw before him a land of lush green plains, bisected by the river that swirled and meandered in a series of muddy ribbons, slowly making its way east toward Kannapolis Lake. This was the home of the Cheyenne, the most powerful of the plains Indians in Colorado. He looked around, hoping to make the town before nightfall, and the lowering sun made long shadows of him and his horses as he rode into what was little more than a small settlement, with the usual cross section of streets that housed the population of a few hundred souls.

He rode into the town off a slight rise and was greeted with friendly smiles by all there. He found a livery barn, agreed a price for his horses and was sent to the only rooming house in the town where he would find a bed for the night. The man and wife who ran it were friendly enough and directed him to the town's only saloon for food.

"Sorry not to be able to oblige, mister, but we don't run to no food, 'ceptin' breakfast, which comes with the price. You'll get a good hot meal at the saloon, though. They'll see you right."

"I'm obliged to you both. I'll make my way there." He

tipped his hat and headed for the Feathers saloon. It was getting crowded as he pushed inside, checking all who were there as was his custom. He saw a couple of tables occupied by men of a certain type, with the wolflike wariness of gunmen. They looked to the uninitiated like cowhands, but they were not. Nate thought that if they did handle cattle they would be rustled, not legal stock. He marked them but made no eye contact, not seeking trouble. At the bar he ordered a beer and a plate of stew. He ate carefully, keeping one hand free and watching the room, sensing that the hard looking men were not of the town, but like himself were passing through. There was a quiet tension to the place, with sideways glances being cast.

Another two men gave him room at their table as they nursed a couple of beers. One was a homesteader by his clothes, the other a storekeeper, and by their looks, they could have been brothers.

"I'm obliged," Nate began, exploring the situation as carefully as he could. "I'm not sure I'd be appreciated at those other tables." He nodded with a smile after he wiped his mouth with the back of his hand.

"You called it right there, mister," the steader replied, below the level of the ambient conversation so as not to be overheard. "Their sort have been driftin' in from time to time over the last week or so and movin' on sharpish, like the next day. Don't pay 'em no mind, this is normally a friendly little town."

"So what draws them here?"

"Not here, exactly. They're headin' off north, where they say there's trouble brewing."

"Really? Hope it's not where I'm headed. I'm looking for a town called Langtonville. I hope to meet up with an old acquaintance there." The two brothers, if that's what they were, exchanged glances and Nate liked none of it.

"If I was you, mister, I'd find friends to call on somewhere else," the storekeeper added. "From what I hear, that's just where they're all headed. There's trouble brewin' over that way, and someone's hiring more of it."

"Now that's a shame," Nate said mildly. "What sort of trouble? If I know then hopefully, I can avoid it. My old acquaintance is very pretty, you see." He smiled.

"She'd better be, because from what I hear this is land trouble. Miners and cattlemen, killings and nesters all thrown together. The town's taking sides and is going to bust wide open from what we hear," he warned.

"Well, I've never been up this way before, so it's all new country to me. I just came up with a cattle drive and thought I'd go calling and pay my respects before I headed back south."

"Then I wish you luck, friend, and hope that she an' her folks ain't wrapped up in it all." The storekeeper toasted him with his beer.

"Amen to that, sir," Nate responded, giving some thought to all he had heard. He could not imagine a genteel family from back east being caught up in such troubles, and part of him wanted to pass it off as a storm in a teacup. Yet he was not minded to back off, it was not in his nature. He resolved to go there and see what all the trouble was about.

He set off the next morning in the direction indicated by the owners of the boarding house, with a couple of landmarks offered by them in his mind so he'd know he was on the right trail. He pulled off the trail when night fell, going a couple of miles out of his way into uncharted territory, reasoning that if gunfighters were being hired and traveling this way, he did not want to be a part of them or even seen by them. The war and traveling through rough country had made him cautious by nature and he now rode with his loop off his gun and his senses wary.

Two days' later, he crested a rise, with sharp red sandstone mesas to his left and rolling hills to his right. The hills were covered with tall trees and he could hear the sound of a mill or a steam pump across the valley before him. The land was covered in lush grass fed by a series of streams and a river that might have been the Smokey Hill, he didn't know. Either way, he thought, this was prime cattle country; grazing served all year round by a plentiful supply of water, a natural basin protected from the worst excesses of weather and a good climate. "So, what's the trouble in paradise, old horse?" he asked Buck, whom he now sat, patting his neck.

He looked about him, smelling the air, scenting cow and buffalo if he was not mistaken. He must not forget that this was Cheyenne country. He nudged the horses forward into a walk and as he hit the plain, he pushed them into a steady ground eating lope. He edged to the left, westwards away from the main trail that skirted the base of the mesas, looking upwards at the ruins of former abandoned dwellings partly carved into the rock, built by cave dwellers before the Cheyenne moved them out.

The dominant tribe will always push out the weaker one.

It's the way and it's what we're doing now to the Indians, he thought.

He made up his mind to explore a little more, see what sort of dwellings they were and learn as much as he could.

Riding northwest for a while he scouted the country, remembering all the marks and signs that he might need to follow one day. Two huge willows akin to sentinels stood by the passage to all who would cross the river. Then there was a copse of cottonwood trees and limes that offered cool shade by a small pool. Here he stopped to water his horses and refill his canteen. He pulled out some jerky to chew on and stave off his hunger, and thus satisfied he moved on to approach the town from the west. He passed two small ranches, one closer to the trail than the other, and on a hunch he pulled off to see what he could learn about the Harts and if the town ahead was their home.

As he got closer he saw that the setup of the ranch was not dissimilar to his own. The house was set in an L-shape, with smoke rising from the chimney and the smell of baking in the air. A veranda ran the length of the building to the front, and off to the side were two sturdy looking smaller log structures, one of which looked like a bunkhouse. Two corrals stood next to a creek that would meet the river he had just crossed. A row of aspens lined the water, their leaves rustling in the breeze. It was a homely setting and had him thinking of his own ranch back in Texas.

"Hallo the house!" Nate called as he got closer.

The door opened on the porch and a man stepped out, keeping in the shadows, and Nate saw the glint of a gun barrel. "That's far enough, mister. State your business," came the harsh reply.

"Just passing through and came to say howdy and ask directions. Nothing more. I've ridden up from Dodge via Cheyenne Wells and I'm looking for an old acquaintance. I didn't mean to startle you," Nate answered evenly.

He sensed the man's hesitation, torn between the normal good manners of the west and whatever was troubling him.

Another figure, a cowhand by his dress and manner, appeared from the bunkhouse, rifle at the ready.

Nate saw the shadow of a second cowhand behind him. Nate raised his right hand slowly. "Mister, if it's that much trouble I'll just turn around and leave and you can shoot me in the back if you will," Nate responded coolly, nudging Buck around the way he had come, making to walk his horses down the track to the trail.

He had only ridden two strides when the man from the main house hailed again: "Hold it, mister, I'm a little jumpy and no man has been turned away from my house yet without at least a cup of coffee. Get down and set. I apologize for my manners, but we're all wound up a little tight of late." The man was a typical rancher, stocky, and browned by the sun, with the gnarled and calloused hands and the bowlegged gait of a horseman. "S'alright, Bob. We'll be fine." He waved to the cowhand by the bunkhouse.

Nate turned, rode up and dismounted, keeping his movements slow and his hands in sight. "Thank you, mister. I'm obliged."

"I'm Linus Farnham. Apologies for your reception." The man held out his hand and Nate shook it.

Nate smiled winningly: "Nate Carlton, how do you do?"

"Fine, fine. Tie up your horses. The wife's baking and there's some coffee on. Come and join us."

Nate saw to his horses, slackening off the girth and tethering them under a large oak that shaded the corral before walking up to the house. He removed his hat and walked in as the smell of fresh baking became stronger. "Good day, ma'am. Nate Carlton," he greeted the woman before him.

She was about thirty years old and still pretty, not yet beaten down by the rough weather of the plains and the harsh frontier life. She smoothed her hands down her apron and offered one to Nate. "Laura, Laura Farnham. Please take a seat and I'll bring cookies and coffee." She smiled up at him.

"By the looks of things, you folks are expecting trouble."

"It's been happenin'." Linus nodded. "Not to us, but other smaller ranchers around the valley have had trouble. One family was wiped out. Made to look like Indians, but it warn't. Scalped 'em crudely and left 'em for dead, but one lived and told the story before she died. White men dressed up as savages did it. In a word, mister, there's a lot goin' on and some of it puzzles me. When it comes down to it, it's a land grab. Some folks want it, and we aren't giving it to 'em." Linus continued as Nate tucked into his cookie and sipped his coffee, listening to all he said, his concern rising. "We been here ten years, built this place up from nothin'. It's not huge, but it's good land and serves us well. Then someone struck silver in the hills over yonder." He flicked his thumb over his shoulder. "That was the start, then they found gold as well. That blew the town wide open, and it's doubled in size in as many months. With it came new people, buying up land for big cattle spreads and mining and goodness only knows what else. Worse was when Timmins sold his old spread. Man who bought it doubled his size to twelve hundred acres and he wants more.

"The town's changed, too. Three or four businesses sold out to eastern buyers, no one knows who. Prices have gone up with it. It's getting so it's hard to do business."

"Has the town got any law or a council?" Nate asked as his first thought.

"Sure, Andy's been marshal for a few years and acts as deputy sheriff so his jurisdiction goes wider. Him and two deputies are stretched, though. Every Saturday there seems to be a killing down near the miners' tents or somewhere close. He's strugglin' and no mistake. Hardcases have been brought in to protect certain interests. But these gunfighters—least that's the term they use, anyways—they're as bad as the men they've been hired to stop. Some really bad men in town and they're holding sway with new saloons and gambling dens and such. Nate, I hate to say it, but if I was you I'd saddle my horse, see whoever you came to see and get the hell outta here."

"Oh, Linus, don't you just go on? I'm sure Nate here don't want to hear all our woes. Tell us what brought you here, Nate," Laura encouraged him.

"Well, ma'am. I met a girl down Charlottesville way a while ago after I came back from the war. You know how it is, she was very pretty. She invited me to call upon her if ever I was up this way again. I came in with a herd to Dodge, like I was saying to Linus here, and I thought I'd admire to see a bit more country and maybe call upon her to see if she was as pretty as I remember," he finished, smiling at the rancher's wife.

"Well now, don't that sound romantic? So the herds have come in early this year?"

"I do believe that we were the first major herd up the trail, ma'am. Came in about a week ago, brought up nearly two thousand five hundred head of prime beef. It was good drive," he answered proudly.

"Whose herd was it?" Linus asked.

"It was a syndicated drive, but I was the trail boss. We put together all the smaller spreads that couldn't afford to do a drive by themselves, picked up some more through the Nations like we did last year and brought them all in together."

Linus scratched his chin, thinking how young Nate was to be a trail boss. Then it came to him. "Charlottesville, you say? You from South Carolina?"

"Yes I am. At least that's where my parents lived, although they came from England initially."

"Wait. Nate Carlton. Why didn't I think of it before and put two and two together? You're the man who broke Brannigan's bunch of herd cutters and faced down the DR Connected boss in Dodge last year! Why I expected you to be older—no offense."

Laura Farnham looked again at the innocent looking young man with nice manners who sat at her table. She too had heard the stories, rangeland gossip being what it was.

"None taken. Yes, we brought in a herd and it went well.

Had a bit of trouble again this year but they seemed to take the hint and left us alone." He smiled disarmingly.

"You're getting quite a reputation," Linus remarked, looking with interest at Nate's gun belt and holstered guns.

"Well, if it's to do with anything but cattle it's not one I would seek or encourage," Nate replied firmly.

Laura broke the slight tension that had arisen. "What's the name of this young lady who took your eye, Nate?"

"Her name is Isobel Hart. Her father ranches out here, so I am led to believe. Do you know her?"

The husband and wife exchanged glances. "Son, that's the name of the man who has been buying the land. The one who bought Timmins's spread," Linus said. "If you're going to side with him then we'd best part company right now, nice as you seem. And I hope that you ain't been sent to spy on us," he added, anger and suspicion appearing in his voice once more.

Chapter Four

Nate left the Farnham homestead under a cloud. It looked like suspicion had followed him as he had ridden down the trail to their house, and he wondered what the Hart family had done that had set them at such odds with the township. Though he had never met Isobel's father, she—and even her stuck up mother—had seemed decent, law abiding citizens straight out from the east. What would they know about land grabbing and putting together a large cattle spread? Something in his mind wasn't making sense, although he admitted to himself that not all villains and evil doers looked like Craw Gillett, the man who had stolen and taken over his parents' estate as part of the Reconstruction after the war.

He rode the last few miles into town and slowed to a walk as he entered the limits. In the distance he saw the steam rising from where a tented city of miners had settled. Tents dotted the lower slopes of the hills behind the town. A painted sign read Langtonville, Population (and here it had been crossed out a few times) 3,561.

A growing town, he mused. *I wonder how many will stay when the mines are all worked out?*

The town was built on a grid system as he'd expect, but the main street had new buildings running off it at ninety degrees to form a crossroads. The gaudy fronts of saloons, hotels and gambling houses occupied the prime positions at the crossroads, with new buildings evident where an older structure had been pulled down to widen the street. It was a radical move which implied that whoever did it had faith in the growth of the town.

He looked up as he rode closer down the wide main street at the sign for the Golden Deuce saloon. Fair name, he considered. The tinkling of a piano drifted out from the buildings as he glimpsed a couple of dance hall girls moving around inside. By the noise, it was already doing fair business. It was getting near to sundown and being a Saturday a few cowpunchers had come in early, newly paid and keen to lose their money at the various attractions that the town had to offer.

He moved on down Main Street, seeing how the premises changed with the character of the area. Every town had a rhythm, he knew, and beyond the center, trees had been planted around structures that were clearly residential. This would be the older, more established part of the town. A boarding house with a neat picket fence came next with a hitch rail outside. A sign outside read: Kim's Boarding House. Rooms and Meals. Nate dismounted, deciding it was as good a place as any he had seen and it would be quieter away from the noise of the saloons and dance halls farther along the street. He dismounted, hitched Buck and Patch, brushed off the dust of the trail and stepped onto the porch to open the door. The action rang a bell above, and the first thing Nate smelled was lavender, which reminded him of home. To one side was a dining area with two trestle tables and chairs offering food for guests. Drapes hung at the windows and the place seemed homely and clean.

A matronly woman appeared from a back office or kitchen, her hair pulled back in a tight bun. Her face was stern but kindly and seemed to suit the aura of the place. She looked him up and down, noticing that he removed his hat.

"Evening, ma'am," Nate said. "I was wondering if you had any rooms to rent and a hot meal."

"Good evening," she responded. "I may do. How long are you planning on staying?"

"I don't really know yet. I'm looking for an old acquaintance and I'm not sure how lucky I'll be. Maybe three or four days?"

"Uh-huh. That'll be a dollar a night and food on top if you eat here. I can do your laundry too. Rooms are upstairs and I like them kept clean and no visitors after dark, if you know what I mean." Here she raised an eyebrow.

"I do indeed, ma'am."

"Good rooms. The sheets are clean, and I like 'em to stay that way. There's a bath house out back and I wish more would use it. I can get hot water if you've a mind to use one."

"Ma'am, that sounds like a fine idea to me."

She broke into a smile then offered her hand to be shaken. "Good. My name's Kim."

"Nate Carlton. How do you do?"

Kim frowned. "Do I know that name?"

"Don't think so, ma'am. I've never been this way before."

She looked hard at him again, trying to place the name in her memory, then she gave up and shouted over her shoulder. "Ying, get some hot water, man here wants a bath."

A Chinese man appeared in the doorway, bowed and scuttled off.

"Thank you. I'll see to my horses and be right back."

Nate asked directions to the best livery barn and rode into town to look for it after leaving his warbag and bedroll at Kim's.

With the horses settled he walked back, carrying his rifle, looking at all the buildings and enjoying the bustle of a booming new town. There were four saloons near the crossroads, three gaming houses, a dance hall, three restaurants and three cathouses that he counted. Oil lamps were being lit and the noise was growing louder.

He called in at the Northern Star saloon for a beer to take away the dust of the trail. He pushed open the doors to the bright lights of the saloon, which was much better appointed than most frontier establishments, with curtains, a chandelier, gambling and a partitioned dining area with tables laid out for food off to the side. The bar gleamed and was already busy with a typical cross section of customers, from storekeepers to cowboys as well as a few hardcases who leaned over the bar. They all gave him the once over as he entered.

He walked across to the bar, avoiding the eyes of the pretty saloon girls who were working the floor and ordered a beer. A frothy glass appeared, and he drank swiftly.

"Well, that surely hit the spot," he said to the barman, a

beefy man with a florid red face and a shiny multi-colored satin vest.

"Glad to hear it, friend. Traveled far?" he enquired, which was within the realms of western etiquette. The barman was curious, the newcomer was well set up with a fancy rig and a tied down gun, yet he didn't have the wolfish, hard eyed look of a gunman.

"Just came up with a herd from Texas and thought I'd see a bit of the country before heading back down south." Something warned him about saying more, and he left it there. The barman served another customer between polishing glasses, then exchanged a few more words with Nate. "Not looking to settle here or work, then?" he asked.

Nate was aware that the conversation was being listened to by others at the bar and was equally cautious. "No, just passing through. Be here for a couple of days and then I'll move on." He smiled and continued to sip his beer.

A couple of hardcases looked on with interest, clearly on the prod and out for entertainment. "That's a good idea, partner. The climate here ain't healthy for strangers who stay too long," one said, looking pointedly at him.

Nate smiled genially to avoid trouble and said: "Much obliged for the advice." He finished his beer and placed the empty glass back on the bar, thanked the barman, turned and left.

The hardcase was puzzled, expecting a strongly worded response, then laughed with his friend. "Seems like he don't like our company. Got all the fancy gun rig but can't back it up."

"If you boys are going to scare away all the customers,

why don't you do it in someone else's saloon?" The barman snarled at them.

"Yeah, or what?" the hardcase retorted.

"Or I'll have you removed and left in the gutter for dead," came a soft voice from behind them. Turning, the hardcase looked at the double barrel of a Derringer pistol held rock steady in the manicured hand of a beautiful woman. For a saloon girl, her dress was tasteful and decorous, although it was cut low over the chest exposing more decolletage than any townswoman would dare to show. When she moved the long gown was shown to be split to mid-thigh, exposing a perfect stockinged leg and a red garter. The face above the dress was glamorous but hard, and the china blue eyes that had seen most things the world had to offer were set off by a pile of exquisite red hair.

"Alright, Candy, we ain't arguing. We're only funning," the man muttered, raising his hands.

"Well go fun somewhere else or behave. I ain't lookin' for any trouble in here," the woman purred. Her tone was soft, but there was menace in every word.

To back her up, the barman produced a sawn off shotgun and a faro dealer had left his position to show his holstered Colt, his jacket drawn back ready to back Candy's play.

"No argument from me, Candy, I'll be good."

"See that you do. Bill, give the man a drink, I guess his nerves prob'ly need it." With that she swept past them, the Derringer disappearing as she went out through the saloon doors. Her heels clicked on the sidewalk as she caught up to Nate in a few quick strides.

"Hey, mister, wait. I don't like my customers being frightened off," she called after him.

Nate turned, and seeing her he could not resist a smile at the glamorous woman who was swishing towards him. "Well, ma'am," he said, touching his Stetson. "I certainly appreciate the effort on my behalf. But I'd finished my beer and his kind will always try to find a reason to cause trouble, so I thought I'd leave before they did. I just want a peaceful life."

"I admire your restraint. I know fine what you can do. I saw you in Dodge last year when you faced down David Randall and I heard the story about Brannigan's gang. You're welcome in my saloon any time, Mister Carlton." Her voice was seductive, and she lowered her eyes in a provocative manner as she extended her hand. "I'm Candy Tryst and I run the Northern Star."

"Candy, how do you do? I appreciate the offer and I'll maybe come back later, especially if the food is good. In the meantime, I surely would appreciate it if you didn't blast my name around. Just Nate will do fine."

"The food is good, I have a French chef, and I will mind what you say. Nate it is." Her grip was firm and dry when she shook his hand. She smiled and turned away, her hips swaying as she walked back into the saloon.

Nate grinned to himself. *Oh my,* he said to himself. *That's quite a woman there, Nate, quite a woman.*

On his way back to Kim's, Nate saw the marshal's office down one of the roads that crossed the main street and called in to introduce himself and obtain some information.

"Howdy, marshal," he said, pushing open the door to the jailhouse and office.

A lean man around forty years old sat behind the desk. He was dressed in neat, well-worn town clothes with a string tie at his neck and a serviceable Adams revolver at his hip. He had a tan that bespoke as many hours out of his office as in it.

The marshal looked up from his ledger with shrewd dark eyes that looked Nate over, noting his armament. Undeterred, Nate continued. "I just got into town today and wanted to introduce myself and ask for some information, if I may? I decided that this would be the best and most honest way to obtain it."

"Well, I like a man who comes to me first for information," the marshal replied. "Saves me having to worry about who he is and what he wants. Lord knows I've enough trouble in town as it is."

"I can see that. Seems a man just has to look the wrong way in this town, even minding his own business, he can get into a fight. You've certainly got your work cut out."

"That I have. I'm Andy Gorringe, marshal of Langtonville. Now, what can I do for you mister....?"

"Carlton. Nate Carlton," he said shaking Gorringe's hand and waiting for a reaction. All he got was a searching glance and a raised eyebrow. If the marshal recognized the name he wasn't giving anything away.

"I came up with a herd into Dodge," Nate continued, "and pushed on north hoping to meet with an acquaintance, lady by the name of Isobel Hart. Do you have any idea where I might find her? I understand that her father owns a cattle ranch around here but given what I've seen, I didn't want to set tongues wagging or offer my services to what might just turn out to be the wrong side."

"Well, that's a wise move. I'll give you that. Hart, you say? Don't got nothin' against Miss Isobel, but bandying that family's name around will get you either friends or enemies, maybe a bit of both. Her father bought a spread out west of here towards Denver and he just bought out the old Timmins's place. Now he's got himself upward of four thousand acres of prime land. The ranch is called the Circle Hart. You head northwest for about eight miles or so and you'll meet the main trail. Keep going for about a mile west after you see two big old oaks where the trail forks. You'll come to a rise. When you get to the ridge you'll see a basin and there she'll be, you can't miss it."

"I'm much obliged to you. I'm just curious here, so tell me to mind my own business, but do you run this town by yourself?"

The marshal snorted in mock amusement. "Nope. I got me two deputies, and I also act as deputy sheriff, so my jurisdiction goes outside the town boundaries. They'll be along soon, and tonight will be busy as it's Saturday, with cowboys on one side and miners on the other, nesters in between and townsfolk caught in the middle. Watch how you go now, it gets a bit lively from time to time."

Nate nodded. "Well, thank you once again. I'll see you around, marshal." Nate tipped his hat and left the office. He saw a new saloon sign outside what was currently no more than a huge tent, with lumber works going on all around it. The sign boasted: cheap whisky, good beer and honest gambling in the Barrel saloon, and was signed by the proprietor, Shaun McCrae.

Everyone had heard of Shaun McCrae. He had come down from the Barbary Coast via the riverboats and mining camps and had gained a reputation as an evil man with a mean reputation for killing and running roughshod over anyone who got in his way. Nate shook his head in disgust; he could imagine that the cheap whisky would taste exactly like what it was—something that had been badly distilled in a back shed behind the tent.

Other tented saloons and gaming houses were evident, all providing temptation for the unwary and anyone who wanted to get liquored up at the end of a hard day. The town was attracting the worst elements, and Nate knew that one day soon all the tensions would boil over, driving the good people away and leaving the rough shell of what had once been as the mines bottomed out, which they would, Nate knew. He'd passed through other towns that had seen this boom and bust before the war, and he didn't envy the marshal or his deputies keeping the lid on this simmering kettle.

Bathed, dressed, and feeling hungry, Nate made his way down to the guesthouse dining area, where he ate a hearty meal and stayed talking with Kim and a couple of other residents over coffee. He wanted an early start in the morning, and learned as much as he could about what was going on in the town and the surrounding area.

As far as he could tell, none of it was good.

Chapter Five

The next day Nate made an early start. He saddled up Patch after breakfast and leaving Buck to rest he rode off northwest following the directions given to him by Marshal Gorringe. He found the main trail and the turn by the two large oak trees and forked left as he had been instructed. It was very pretty country, full of long, deep valleys, lush grass and most importantly fed by lots of streams and small lakes. Trees lined the lakes, and on the gently sloping banks of hills there were bristlecone pine, spruce and cottonwood.

It would be good country for cattle, and the red sandstone mesas lining his way followed a natural formation to the west. Nate imagined it would be a wild and untamed country beyond them and made up his mind to explore it before he left to go south. He kept an eye open for Indians, as this would be good hunting lands for them, and the Cheyenne would not give them up without a fight. Checking tracks he saw evidence of unshod ponies, traveling light and in a group, moving in the same direction as him before veering off to the east.

He followed the trail upwards, and as he came to the crest he looked down into a basin below, in which a large ranch house, corrals, a bunkhouse and various barns and outbuildings had been built. He stopped to look at the setting, taking it all in. The house was on a slight rise, set back against the lee of a shallow hill that rose gently northward. A row of poplars stood like custodians, protecting the house from the north wind, and he caught the sweet scent of them on the breeze. It was, he decided, an idyllic picture. He nudged Patch forward, riding down the trail to the arched entrance of the ranch, a sign burned into a wooden plaque denoting it the Circle Hart Ranch.

As he got closer he heard whoops of encouragement as a cowhand tried to stay on a bucking horse in the round pen. He lost the battle as Nate watched, flying through the air to land hard and roll away before he was stomped on by the aggressive bronco. Two other cowhands moved in to catch the errant animal and it was then that his presence was noticed. The group turned as one to look him over. Not all were friendly in their stares, Nate noticed, and they looked like a mixed bunch, he decided. Some of the men turned to the side, their hands hanging negligently near their guns, menace and unfriendliness in their attitude.

"Howdy," Nate called in a friendly manner, pulling up his dark silk blue bandana to mop his brow, taking time to see everything about him and assess the situation.

A lean figure came forward, low hanging gun by his side, loop off and gun tied down.

"You're on Circle Hart land. We ain't hiring and whatever it is you've got, we don't want any," the man said abruptly.

It was not what Nate had expected. "Well now, that's good, means I can still read properly. It's also lucky, because I'm not for hire and I'm not selling anything," he said gently, with no arrogance in his manner. He didn't like the man before him or his attitude.

It took the speaker a few seconds to recover. "Then get. We don't like strangers here and you ain't welcome."

"How about we let Miss Hart decide that? I'm here at her invitation and I'm minded to call on the house and see her, if that's alright with you."

The lean man was taken aback by the use of Isobel Hart's name but continued aggressively. "And if it ain't? 'Cause you're takin' in a mighty wide loop of country, mister."

"Knock it off Chas, leave him be." The voice came from a stocky man in cowhand clothes who came from the barn. He was in his mid-forties and tough looking, and although he had none of the arrogance of the other man, he carried the stamp of authority. "I'm Dave Brannon, foreman of the Circle Hart. You want to see Miss Isobel?" he asked suspiciously, wondering why a lone stranger would be invited to meet the boss's daughter.

Nate smiled in response, turning to Brannon and deliberately ignoring Chas. "Indeed. We met on a riverboat down near Charleston and she invited me to call upon her if I was in the neighborhood. I just came up this way with a herd from Texas and thought I'd see some country and call on Miss Isobel."

"Well, mister, you sure are a long way from home. Step down and follow me to the house."

Nate tipped his hat. "I'm obliged. Nate Carlton," he introduced himself.

There was some low muttering from the men, and Brannon raised an eyebrow. "You're Nate Carlton? From South Carolina?"

"One and the same," Nate offered.

"Uh huh," was all Brannon said in response. "Well follow me and I'll take you to the main house. How was the drive up?" he asked, changing the subject.

"Oh, fair. Hot, dusty, a stampede, herd cutters, the usual stuff," he replied.

"Yep, that'd be about right. You did well, we heard about the Carlton Syndicate herd. Great idea for the small ranchers. We're busy building a large spread here, too."

Nate confirmed that he had, and on the walk up to the house they talked cattle drives and ranching as one cowman to another in the easy manner of their kind.

Back at the corral, the conversation started. "You hear that, Al," one cowboy said. "That's Nate Carlton, the one who broke up Brannigan's bunch."

"Well, he don't seem much to me," Chas responded. "Just a wet behind the ears kid, seems like."

Up at the house Nate loosened the cinch on Patch, tied him to the hitching rail, swept off his hat and rubbed his forehead again. He was suddenly nervous. It had been a while since he'd had any conversation with a good looking woman who wasn't a dance hall girl and he wondered if Isobel would remember him.

He walked up the steps onto the porch of the large house, where Brannon knocked and went in, removing his own hat as he did so, leading Nate into a wide hall that was cool and airy. Drapes hung at the windows, a grandfather clock chimed at the side of the hall and a mahogany occasional table that had been polished to a high sheen bore a vase of fresh cut flowers. It was an elegant home, Nate thought, not dissimilar to his own former home in South Carolina.

Light footsteps echoed along the floorboards, and then she appeared. She looked lightly tanned and was as pretty as Nate had remembered. Her freckles were more pronounced and her copper colored hair, streaked with gold bleached by the sun, was caught in a clasp at the nape of her neck. Her eyes were the same blue, and Nate decided that she looked even prettier than the last time he'd seen her.

"Miss Isobel, this here is Nate—"

"Nate? You came! How lovely to see you," she gushed.

"Well, Miss Hart. I'm mighty pleased to be here." Nate twirled his hat between his fingers, suddenly nervous again.

"Well, I'll leave you two alone to get reacquainted." Dave smiled.

Just then another voice was heard, speaking in a cultured eastern accent. "Who is it, dear?"

"Mama, you remember Nate from the riverboat in South Carolina? We met him on the way to see Aunt Jenny in Charleston."

Mrs. Hart frowned a little as she walked into the room. Stretching her memory, it was obvious to Nate that she had no real desire to succeed. Then she recalled, sniffed disdainfully and continued: "Yes, that awful altercation on the riverboat. Two men were killed as I recall. How do you do, ...mister...?"

"Carlton, ma'am. Nate Carlton. How do you do?"

"Yes, quite so. Well, Mr. Carlton, do please come through to the parlor and I shall arrange for coffee to be served." She turned her back and linked her arm through Isobel's. *Oh dear,* Nate thought, *worse than I remembered.*

As Dave Brannon was leaving he smothered a smile, winked surreptitiously at Nate, mouthed good luck and made himself scarce, closing the door to the lion's den behind him.

Nate followed the two women, taking in the stately elegance of the room and the comfortable furnishings. Mrs. Hart indicated one of the smaller couches and invited him to sit. He found himself sinking into a well upholstered seat.

Mrs. Hart, satisfied that her daughter's virtue was safe, left to order coffee from the housekeeper.

Through an open door to a side room came a man's rich deep voice. "Who was that, darling? Did I hear visitors? I'm expecting my banker today."

"No, Daddy, it's not your banker. Come and meet Nate Carlton from South Carolina."

A tall, bluff figure appeared in the doorway. His stomach pushed against the silver silk of his vest. His face had jowls, but he looked well fed and prosperous. He was gently tanned, at odds with his townie appearance, and had a mane of dark hair that was slicked back and showed a few streaks of grey at the temples that suited him, giving him an air of gravitas. His shrewd, deep-set eyes appraised

Nate, who felt he was being pierced with an all-knowing glare.

Nate responded with good manners, standing from the overstuffed couch and offering his hand to shake. "Good morning, sir, how do you do?" he said.

"Good morning. Have you just arrived?" he asked, noting Nate's clothes and armament.

"Yes, I rode up from Langtonville this morning to call upon your daughter. I hope I'm not intruding."

"Not at all, but I do have an important meeting with my banker and I'm expecting him shortly, so you will have to excuse me as I have papers to prepare. Are you staying long in the area?"

"I hadn't decided, sir. I'll have to return to Texas at some point in the near future and look to my affairs down there, but I was hoping to see Isobel first before I leave."

"And what affairs would they be?" Hart asked rudely. "Rounding up cattle?"

"Something of that nature, yes," Nate answered ambiguously. He was damned if he was going to play a game of one-upmanship with the pompous snob he saw before him. "Well, sir, if you're expecting company I won't delay you any further," Nate added.

Isobel rose. "Oh, but you *must* stay for coffee," she said, making it more of a command than a request. "Mama has just gone to organize some, and it would be lovely to show you the ranch." She smiled innocently at her father, who offered her a non-committal grunt and stalked back to his study. She rolled her eyes when he had gone and mouthed an apology.

Nate smiled in response, putting her at ease. They exchanged a few quiet whispers until her mother returned followed by a maid carrying a tray of coffee and crockery. The next half hour was unmitigated purgatory for Nate, who suffered the stuffy, snobbish and patronizing stings of Mrs. Hart and was frankly glad when the banker called, giving him the opportunity he needed to take his leave.

Yet Isobel was not to be put off, showing her strength of character by offering to walk him to his horse. She swept out before her mother could object, with Nate following in her wake. She showed him a little of the ranch and they stole a few moments together before she told him that he had better leave. "Listen, we go to town on Tuesday, can I see you then?"

"I should like that very much," Nate replied. He kissed her cheek, tightened the cinch, mounted his horse and tipped his hat. "I'll be at Kim's boarding house. I shall look forward to next Tuesday." He wheeled Patch and walked him down the driveway, passing the bunkhouse and corrals. As he did so there were jeers from the group of hardcases there, including Chas, who called out: "Did the little lady enjoy your visit, sonny?" To which there was laughter and wolf calls.

He ignored them, but he was puzzled by the mix of gunmen and genuine ranch hands who were there to work the cattle. Each side usually had little to do with the other, with their relationship marked by mutual contempt. There was something about Circle Hart Ranch that didn't add up.

Chapter Six

Nate's ride back to town was uneventful, and with the promise of seeing Isobel again, he decided to stay on in Langtonville, trying to understand more about the town and what was going on.

Various hardcases hung around the saloons, some employed by them as protection against hooraying in the premises. There were a number of factions, many hanging around the Barrel saloon, loafing and looking for trouble. There were a few more stationed at the mines, keeping guard. Then there were the men from the Hart ranch and other, smaller homesteads. It added up to a lot of gunmen and a lot of potential trouble.

On the following morning, Nate left Kim's for the Square Deal restaurant to get a cup of coffee. As he walked he became aware of someone beside him as Marshal Gorringe fell in by his side.

"Howdy, mind if I tag along?" he asked casually.

"Free country, I'm off to get a coffee. Would you care to join me?"

"I would indeed," Gorringe answered.

The restaurant was clean and well looked after, with a good menu, and when the two men had made themselves comfortable with their backs to the wall at the far end, the marshal began.

"I hear that you made it to the Hart place and met Chas Doorman yesterday?"

"I sure did, news travels fast. I met Miss Hart, but I had a frosty welcome from her family, I must say."

"Well, I ain't that surprised. The old man made a lot of money in the war with munitions and suchlike. He got pretty rich. He's new money from Boston and Mrs. Hart is old money and likes everyone to know it. You'll get little slack there, I can tell you now."

"I could feel the icy blast from where I was sitting," Nate joked. "Though I was warned about the reception by Doorman. What's the story there, with gun hands and cowboys mixing on the same ranch? Seems very odd. I reckon some of those gunnies haven't done a day's ranching in their lives, and they sure as hell didn't look like they were there to learn."

"You got it. Tell you the truth I don't know the answer for sure. There have been raids on smaller ranches. One attack was made to look like Indians, another family forced out, they just packed a wagon and up and left. I don't know what drove them out. There are three more reasonable sized spreads around, all with tough crews who don't scare easy. But it's one thing to ride for your brand and another to shoot it out with paid gunmen. Then there's the mines, all beavering away fetching motherlodes of silver and gold out of the hills—but here's the joke, they can't ship it out."

"Why not?" Nate asked.

"Stage line won't do it. Too risky, they say. One guard ain't enough. They reckon that there's upwards of about a hundred maybe a hundred and fifty thousand dollars' worth to be shipped. That's a mighty temptin' haul just with one guard to ride shotgun and no one else to do it. Rumor has it that the camps of gun hands are just waiting for the first run. A small one was stopped, passengers robbed, one wounded and the driver let go with just two horses and no guns. Someone leaked information and it'll happen again as sure as eggs are eggs if they try to ship a bigger load.

"Then there's Indians. The Lord only knows what they'll do. Put all this together with the good sites in the town being taken for saloons and gambling houses and we all know what else, and then there's nesters determined to hang onto their smallholdings. Some of 'em have got some mighty pretty spots too. Well-tended, good grass and water. They're good solid people who have been around since the town was nothing but a few stores and a wide space on the trail.

"So the town is standing still, stagnating if you will, but getting ready to blow its lid. Something will happen, you mark my words, either in the town or someplace near it. I can't be in three places at once and I've only got two deputies."

"So why tell me?" Nate asked. "I mean it's good to know, but I'm just here visiting a girl."

"I thought about that. Two things. First, you came in

here honestly and you clearly ain't here on the prod, and second you went to see the Harts and came back in one piece. Now, I got no proof of it, just suspicions, and I'm sure old man Hart benefited from Timmins selling to him. He's now the biggest landowner around here, and from what I hear he wants more beef. That means he'll need more land to put 'em on. But the land's all taken, so where's he goin' to get it from?"

"But how does that tie in with everything else you have told me?"

"I don't know. I'm trying to figure it out my own self."

"But you still haven't told me why I should be interested," Nate asked.

"Well, I was wondering if you could see your way clear to helpin' me out, on the quiet like, unofficially. Try to see what's goin' on out of town. You're an honest man, trusted with ranchers' herds, and you've got a way in to Hart's spread and it don't look to me like you're scared of much."

What? You want me to spy for you?" Nate asked incredulously.

"Not in so many words. Just ride around see what you can find, who's out there lurking."

"Why not just send for a U.S. Marshal?"

"I have, but they tell me they can't spare another one without a good reason. A booming town ain't enough. By the time something happens, it'll be too late."

Nate looked at the marshal over the rim of his coffee cup, squinting his eyes against the rising steam. "I can't say I like your reasons for involving me, but I also feel for you. I'll tell you what I'll do. I'll ride around in the normal course of my life, if I see anything suspicious—tracks, unusual groups and so forth—I will report back to you. But as to sticking my nose in where it's not wanted, no, I won't do that. I didn't come here looking for trouble," he said emphatically.

"Son, I can't ask for more. I appreciate it more than you know, and it would be doing me a big favor. Because you're not on the books I can't pay you in dollars, but I guess I could buy you something you might need and charge it to the town tab?"

Nate was about to say no, then he thought about something that had been nagging him for a couple of days. He had not been practicing for a week or so with his gun. "I'll tell you what, you can buy me some boxes of cartridges and bullets for my six guns, how does that sound? I also need to find somewhere to practice unseen, do you have any suggestions?"

"Done on the cartridges. And there's a small shootin' range behind the gunsmith's shop. Always gunfire comin' from there so a bit more won't draw a comment. I'll have a word with Cliff, he'll likely let you use it. If that's too close then there's a draw off the trail heading towards the red mesa west of here. It looks like a game trail but it dead ends in a box canyon. No one really goes there. It's quiet and the sound won't carry as far as here. That suit you?"

"Thank you, marshal. I appreciate it. I'll try the gun store tomorrow and see how I go."

They talked a little more, then Nate made his excuses and left. He saddled Buck this time and rode out to try to find the draw that the marshal had described. It took him half an hour before he found it between two small boulders that almost disguised the trail. He had some wooden boxes of cartridge cases left and a fully loaded spare cylinder that he kept in his saddle bag wrapped tightly in an oiled cloth. He swapped the cylinders regularly to keep them from wearing unevenly and to keep the loads in good shape.

He tied the holster to his thigh and saw two pinecones still on a tree. He settled himself, drew, and fired. Both cones exploded in a shower of chips. He found more and continued until the gun was empty. Then he dropped, closing his eyes, pulled the lever, emptied the cylinder, brought the new one up and settled it, locked it in place, span it and continued with his practice. For an hour he drew and fired from different positions, alternating between the Police and Navy Colts, practicing the Border Shift, the Road Agent's Spin and everything Sam had taught him.

A new thought had occurred on the drive up when he saw one of the hands pull a Colt lefthanded from a cavalry twist holster, drawing and shooting to kill a rattler. It had not been exceptionally fast, but it was smooth, and it got Nate to wondering if he could use his left hand to draw the smaller Colt. The belt holster was set up for a right handed cross draw, but it could work, he decided. He tried and found it clumsy. He discovered that he had to approach from the top, rather than the side, rotate his elbow outward and scoop the gun out, not pull it upwards. With a few tries it became easier and more natural. He carried on practicing for half an hour until he was satisfied that he could do it smoothly, if not as fast as his right handed draw.

Then he turned away back to the horse, and upon an unheard command he dropped, span and drew. The Navy flew into his hand as though on a spring and cord, defying sight. A final narrow branch with a cone hanging from it sheared off, and as the cone fell to the ground, it too exploded into bits. Nate smiled to himself. *There's the edge back,* he thought. He flipped the gun upward to spin in the air, caught it left-handed, fired twice more left-handed, flipped a Border Shift, did a twist draw, shot again at a small sapling and span both guns to holster them again.

That will do, he thought with a grin. A gun was a tool like any other, and Nate knew that if it was to be used well, it needed constant practice. He took each gun out in turn, ejecting the spent paper cartridges, reloaded and set new nipple caps upon the new loads. He undid the pigging thong for his leg, slipped on the hammer thong and prepared to mount up. As he did so, he had that feeling of being watched again and looked around carefully. Scoping out the tops of the mesas, he saw a flicker of light reflected off a glass. As suddenly as it appeared, it was gone. Nate marked the spot. *Too far for a rifle shot he thought, so I'm safe enough*, but he wondered who it was all the same.

Up on the mesa top, Linus Farnham pushed himself back on his stomach, annoyed with himself at being seen by the reflection of his field glasses. "Damn fool thing to do," he muttered, "like some greenhorn. So you're just a cowhand passing through to see a girl, huh, Mister Nate Carlton? Yeah, and I'm the chief of the Cheyenne. What are you doing here what exactly are you practicing for?" He mused on these questions as he rode back to his spread, driving a few stray cattle before him that he had come out to round up.

He was still lost in thought as Nate pulled out from a side draw, quietly appearing on the trail in front of him. He had doubled back out of sight, picked up Farnham's tracks and followed them to find out who had been watching. "Howdy, Linus," he said gently.

"Nate Carlton! You sneaking up on me like that damn near scared me out of ten years' growth," Farnham shouted to cover his embarrassment.

Nate flicked a smile across his face. "Well, it looks as though I wasn't the only one sneaking around," he said pointedly, looking at the field glasses slung over the pommel of Farnham's saddle.

"I heard all the shooting and it sounded for all the world like war had been declared again," Farnham blustered.

"Just keeping in practice. A man carries a gun he should know how to use it," he said.

"Yeah, guess so. Did you find your girl, Isobel Hart?"

"I did, thank you. I went to her ranch." Sliding in alongside Linus he pushed a cow back into line as it threatened to break off. It was neatly done, by instinct, showing a cattleman who was good at his job.

Linus was impressed, despite himself. It was not a fancy move, but it showed that Nate knew what he was doing.

"I'm curious, though," Nate continued. "When I got there I saw a mix of cowhands and gunnies. It seemed odd. Some looked like they were running the show, although they were bossed by the foreman, Dave Brannon."

"Like I told you the other day, everyone's been hiring gun hands. Dave, now he's solid. Hart inherited him along with the ranch, which he bought just after the war. He kept on some of the old hands, too, then they started bringing in more of the type who don't fit. They tend to stay over at Timmins's old place." He pointed southwest, over the other side of the mesas. "But they mix with proper cowhands who herd the cattle. They're pushin' and they took over the two homesteads of the couple who just up and left. Rumor has it that there's more cattle comin' in, too."

"I see. Interesting situation," Nate said, as another cow and her calf tried to break out. Nate pushed Buck to a lope, skirted around and pushed her back in line.

"Mister, you ever give up practicing with your guns and want a job herding cows, you just let me know." And for the first time Nate saw a smile crease the older rancher's face.

"I will indeed, sir. But I have enough of my own back down in Texas and another herd to bring up next year, all being well." They were passing through some pretty country, sided by steep hills and mesas, well protected with good grass which Nate commented upon.

"It is worth fighting for, too, and that's what we'll do," Linus stated emphatically.

"A man has to look after his property. You ride around a lot, have you seen any groups of strange riders, tracks, or things out of place?"

Linus gave him a hard look: "Why d'you ask?"

"Marshal Gorringe asked me to keep a look out for him, as a sort of favor."

"Marshal Gorringe? He's a good man, but why you?"

"Said I was new around here, no loyalties or ties." Nate shrugged.

"Well, I guess now that you mention it I have seen some

things. Two different sets of tracks, off to the north on the boundary with the Circle Hart. There's a canyon, big red sandstone sits just off the trail to Denver. Lots of draws there and unknown land. Saw a group of riders' tracks, criss-crossed over the trail and difficult to make out, but odd all the same."

"Thank you. I might take a ride out that way and take a look."

"Uh huh. Listen, afore you go back, would you like a coffee and something to eat? We warn't very friendly last time and I'd like to make amends. Seems like you're OK and I guess I misjudged you."

"I should like that, especially if your wife is baking again," Nate responded with a grin.

It was late afternoon when he finally returned to Langtonville, and he had a lot to think about on the way in. He called at the marshal's office and told him about what Linus had said, promising to ride out that way later in the week and take a look.

"I still don't know how long I'll be staying, though. Seems like the Harts have a different opinion of me than their daughter."

"The mother's a snooty old tyrant and looks down her nose at most people around here. Rafe, now, he can be alright on his good days. Comes into town every now and then and visits the Northern Star for a drink and some company." The marshal winked.

Nate laughed. "So, he's not as pious as he makes out? I also saw two more new signs going up as I came in, one on an older building."

"Yep. Taylor sold out and we got ourselves a new telegraph office. Don't know who runs it, though. Bought by a private corporation."

"Interesting times, seems like everything's growing and expanding round here."

"Yep, and I get the feeling like there's a rush of water running down a canyon after a storm, bringing everything with it to crash out right here in this basin. There's growing pressure to get the gold and silver shifted. They're looking to hire help to move it—but who are they going to trust, that's the key?"

"Don't look at me, marshal. I'm a cattleman, and on that note, I'll be off." Nate picked up his hat, nodded to the marshal, bade him good evening and went back to the boarding house for a bath and a good meal.

The town was already lively as the oil lamps came on, a big crowd in already. There was noise from the saloons, and the tension was almost palpable, as if there was a storm coming across the plains pushing a mighty wind before it. Trouble was coming, and Nate had a feeling it would arrive tonight.

Chapter Seven

Washed and changed, Nate lay on his bed and read for a while. After three chapters of his book, he realized he was hungry and headed out for supper and a glass of wine at the Northern Star. He was relaxed yet pleased with the way the day had gone and looked forward to the arrival of Isobel tomorrow.

He hoped that her mother wouldn't be there, and that he'd have the opportunity to speak to Isobel without the overbearing busybody hovering around her. He walked along the main street, noting the loud and lively atmosphere, and went in through the swing doors of the saloon, stepping to the side and looking around. There was a good cross-section of cattlemen, miners, gun hands and townsmen, and the saloon was busy. The marshal was just finishing a cup of coffee in the dining area, and he nodded to Nate and beckoned him over. Nate sensed hard looks from some of the gun hands but ignored them, avoiding their stares. Trying to face them down was a sure way of inviting trouble, and that was the last thing he needed.

Andy Gorringe indicated the man sitting next to him with his thumb. "This here's one of my deputies, Clem Ford. Clem, meet Nate Carlton from South Carolina."

The young deputy offered his hand, sizing Nate up, clearly having heard about him from the marshal. "Howdy. Here for food? If you are, have our table, we'll be leaving soon to do the rounds."

"Lot of noise out there tonight for a Monday," Nate commented.

"Yeah, it's the last day of the month. Cowpokes' been paid, the miners, too. Could get a mite interesting," the deputy replied, looking around.

They chatted for a bit while Nate ordered food and wine from a surprisingly good list. Candy, it seemed, had made good on her promise.

The two lawmen stayed longer than intended, and when Nate's food arrived, he tucked in with gusto. At that point they all heard shooting from down the street, and the saloon went quiet with an air of expectancy as the people in it listened out for more. It was more than the usual hooraying of the town. These was concerted and intense shooting from different weapons on a back and forth basis.

Another man, with a star showing on his vest, poked his head through the doors. "Trouble, Andy," he called and the face disappeared as the doors swung to and fro.

"Looks that way, Tye." The marshal exchanged glances with his deputy, and they rose as one, picking up their rifles that had been leaning against the table.

"See you soon, Nate," Gorringe muttered, putting on his hat to walk out of the saloon, levering a cartridge into his Henry as he went.

The two men left the saloon to a surge of conversation and exchanged glances. Nate wiped his mouth with his napkin and was about to rise when he smelled perfume and saw the glamorous figure of Candy by his side. She was dressed in a sheath of shimmering purple, hair once more piled up on her head and wearing alluring makeup that enhanced her huge eyes. "Well, hey there," she said. "I'm glad I managed to persuade you to come back and try again."

"Yes, ma'am, you surely did, and it was worth the wait. Great food and wine."

"Call me Candy. Ma'am makes me sound like my mother."

"Sure thing, Candy," he replied smoothly. Then they heard more shots, one of which Nate recognized as the deeper bark of a Henry rifle. He looked away from the woman standing in front of him, but not before he saw a worried look flicker across her face. "Candy, if you will excuse me I think I need to find out what's happening out there. I believe the marshal may be in trouble."

"Oh, I'm sure it's just a bunch of drunk miners," she replied, placing a hand upon his shoulder.

"You're probably right, and if that's the case I'll be back before too long. Be obliged if you'd keep my coffee warm and my glass full for when I return," Nate replied charmingly, and brooking no argument he rose, putting on his Stetson as he did so. He made for the door, where he stopped and listened for a moment as he tied his gun down and slipped the thong off the hammer. The next report told him that the shots were coming from the far end of the street toward the tented canopy of the Barrel saloon. The lack of proper walls made it all the more dangerous, as bullets could fly through the canvas without restraint. He made his way down the street, keeping in the shadows and moving cautiously, seeing nothing of the two lawmen.

A muzzle flash came from within the saloon, then it fell quiet. Nate ran down a side alley and came out at the back of the big tent. Something felt wrong here. He was about to walk to the front when he spotted a darker shape against the back of the tent. A man was pulling the canvas taut and making a slit with a sharp knife. It only took him a few seconds, then the knife was replaced with a pistol held at shoulder height. The man peered through the hole he had made and took aim at something- or more likely someone-inside.

Nate could not stand by and watch murder done. On instinct he shouted, "Marshal, watch your back!" As he spoke, Nate dropped to a squat and called out: "Hold it right there, mister, and drop that gun!"

The dark figure turned in surprise, pulling the pistol to face Nate and firing as he did so. The snapshot in the dark missed, cutting the air by Nate's head where his torso had been a second before. Nate responded as he knew he must, loosing off two rounds as one, flame lancing into the night.

The figure grunted and staggered.

Nate ran up, closing the distance at a slant, not wanting to risk another chance to be killed. He need not have bothered; the man was dead. Two more shots sounded within the tent, and then came the sound of a huge explosion out on the hillside near the mines. Nate ran around the front of the tent to the open flap. Inside, one of the deputies was clasping a hand to a shoulder wound while the marshal and the second deputy were covering the crowd.

"Marshal, it's Nate. Don't shoot me by mistake. I think they're making a play for the gold and silver," he shouted urgently.

"Nate, cover us while we back out," Gorringe replied. Then, turning to the crowd, he called out: "Anyone feels lucky, you'll be the first to go, and I can't miss at this range, as those two fellas there will testify." He nodded at two dead men lying on the floor of the saloon, turning the sawdust red with their blood. Slowly they backed away with Nate covering them, both guns now in his hands. Nate looked around, ready for the first man to break. The saloon held maybe fifty men, many with evil expressions, sitting in the heat of the bar, waiting to claim the bounty from a raid probably organized by McCrae, who stood leaning against the bar with his blackthorn walking stick by his side in his right hand. Marshal Gorringe moved to Nate's side, the Henry ready to fire. Nobody wanted to be first man to move, because that man would be the first to die.

Nate had a thought and warned: "I hear any shots after we're out and I'll burn this place to the ground. It'll go up like tinder wood. Believe me, I'll do it." He unhooked an oil lamp in his right hand having returned the Navy to its holster. They shuffled back out of the tent, Nate holding the oil lamp ready.

The marshal looked drawn. "Thanks, Nate. Can you come with us to the mine? I'm down a deputy."

"Sure. Give him your rifle, Tye." The wounded deputy did so and pulled a six gun awkwardly with his left hand.

"Find the doc and get back to the jail. Hold up there, get a shotgun, and don't let anyone in but us," the marshal ordered.

"Sure, Andy," Tye replied weakly, turning back towards the jail holding his shoulder that was leaking dark red blood across his shirt in the pale light of the oil lamps.

Then the marshal shouted that he was requisitioning three of the horses tethered outside the saloon and advised no one to come out until they were gone, or they'd be shot.

The three men pushed the horses out of the town at a slow gallop, following an easily defined trail and relying on the animals' superior night vision not to put a foot wrong. It was less than a mile to the mines and already the sound of gunshots was getting louder, with visible flashes lancing into the darkness.

The road twisted and turned through small copses of trees until the outline of the mining shacks, trestles, wash beds, smokestacks and piles of rubble already extracted from the workings lay before them. Lean-to shacks held miners who were returning fire sporadically, protecting what appeared to be in the darkness to be a solid single-story structure some twenty feet square, with a low palisade wall along the top. More shots were coming from the roof as those defending the building sought to keep the attackers at bay, but even as they watched, dark shadows were moving from cover to cover, creeping up upon the blockhouse. It was a concerted effort, and well organized, and Nate realized that the miners would soon be overrun. They were not hardened gunmen, more used to fighting with fists and boots and kept firearms more for protection and shooting game than fighting in an all-out war.

The marshal, who clearly knew the terrain, motioned right: "It goes up an incline there, most of the shots are comin' from the boulders below. If we can get up there, we'll have 'em like rats in a trap. Come on, there's a side trail." With that he reined his horse to the right, pushing onto a barely discernable track that was partly hidden by bushes in the dark.

Looking up, Nate saw a low escarpment of rock shining brighter under the moonlight than the surrounding vegetation. Shots flashed from a higher level on the other side. "They've got the same idea," Nate shouted, urging on his borrowed horse to keep pace with the marshal, with the second deputy hot on his tail.

Two of the miners below had started to realize their danger too late, turning their long guns on the dark shapes that bobbed and weaved, seeking higher ground on the left hand side of the slope.

They were barely in time, and were saved only by the marshal's knowledge and the speed of the horses up the worn track. They reached the flat top and dropped from the saddle in unison, each man dismounting and Nate his borrowed Winchester in hand.

Literally as their feet hit the floor, men appeared on the other side of the flat top of the escarpment, metal glinting in the night.

Nate didn't hesitate as one of them took a bead on the marshal. His hand flew down, drawing and firing in one smooth motion, ignoring the rifle in his left hand. Flame spat from his Navy towards the leading figure.

The rifleman cried out, but still held his long gun as Nate sent another bullet into him, knocking him backwards. By then Nate was moving. Only a fool stayed still in a night-time firefight where you were easily marked by the flame from the guns that you fired.

Nate moved left and dropped down as another figure appeared, firing two more shots just above the rock as he ran hunched to offer a smaller target. He dropped behind a boulder just as the silhouette of a third man showed, rifle raised for a shot at the deputy. Twice more Nate's gun echoed in the night, the first shot spinning the rifleman around and the second catching him in the turn. He knew from the war that only dead men gave second chances at night, and that every enemy was a danger unless both hands could be seen and no weapons were showing. The gunman let out a sharp cry of pain before dropping heavily to the floor, dead or unconscious.

Nate holstered the Navy, bringing two hands to the rifle, which he realized was one of the new Winchesters. He levered a shell into the breech and clambered over the lip of the escarpment. By his side Marshal Gorringe limped towards him and then dropped and slithered the rest of the way.

"You hit?" Nate asked.

"Got me in the damn fool leg. Don't think it hit the bone, but I reckon the slug's still in there, and hurts like a sonofabitch. You alright, Clem?" he called out to the deputy.

"Yeah, Andy, thanks to Nate here. Damn, that was fast shooting. You sure saved our bacon," Clem said.

Nate nodded, acknowledging the compliment. "Right, let's dissuade these gentlemen from their attack." At which he aimed low and picked off one of the men behind a boulder. He could not bring himself to shoot to kill a man in the back. The Winchester fired high and hit the gunman in the hip, spinning him around, all thoughts of attack forgotten. The man dropped his rifle, whimpering as the bullet slammed into him.

The rifles from the ridge turned and spat at the attackers below. After two shots each, the marshal shouted down: "This is Marshal Gorringe. Hold your fire. Surrender and we'll take you in alive. We hold the whip hand now. Give up or die."

There was a pause from both sides. Then a figure stood slowly, hands raised. "Alright, don't shoot, I give in," the man said.

Two more rose with their hands up, and from the other side of the camp Nate heard saddle leather creak and hoofbeats as the other attackers made their escape under the cover of darkness.

The miners moved cautiously forward, taking all the weapons from the men who surrendered.

"We'll be right down," Gorringe called. He began to push himself up, wincing in pain, and Nate reached down to help and steady him. He looked hard at the younger man: "Nate, I'm much obliged, I really am. That's twice you've saved my bacon tonight. I'd like to thank you properly once this business is sorted and my leg's cleaned up."

"Sure thing, Marshal. You can buy me a fine drop of single malt, or better yet a cognac, if they have it in that fancy saloon down there." He gestured towards the town behind him.

As he did so, Gorringe collapsed, his leg a bloody mess.

Chapter Eight

The room was still and quiet, with the drapes drawn and only a small amount of morning light coming around the edges. The doctor held the marshal's arm and took his pulse at the wrist. The doctor was of his breed, lean, sharp and economical of movement with a detached practical manner.

The patient's eyes flickered open and searched the room, passing over the doctor and coming to rest upon the other two figures present. One was Nate, the other a woman of comely appearance, stern in demeanor with a brisk no nonsense attitude about her, who looked on, studying her patient with concern.

"Good to have you back, marshal," the doctor said, "it was a close run thing, and you lost a lot of blood. Good job that this young fella brought you back when he did and tied a tourniquet around your leg, otherwise you wouldn't have made it."

Gorringe offered a wan smile. "That's three times in one

night, Nate. How bad is it, doc?" he croaked through parched lips.

"I got the bullet out and cleaned the wound, so with rest and good food you should be right as rain in a few weeks. You'll limp for a while but that should clear up," the doctor replied, his tone disapproving. "Now I'm going to have to leave you in the care of Nurse Mallory here, as I have many others to attend to. The town's in quite a mess, one way or another." He wagged a finger as if it was all the marshal's fault. "Don't talk much and go back to sleep. You'll feel drowsy as I've given you some laudanum for the pain. I'll call in later this afternoon."

"Grumpy old fussbudget, he's always been the same," Gorringe said, winking at the nurse. "Some water would be good." The nurse smiled and came forward with a glass, and he sipped slowly at it. "Nate, don't go, need to talk to you."

"Later, marshal. I'll come back after the doctor has seen you later today." Nate nodded and made a swift exit before he could be shooed away by Nurse Mallory, who he had learned was fierce in her ministrations, despite the obvious soft spot she had for Gorringe.

He left the marshal's house that lay just outside the town's main street. Andy Gorringe was a widower, and the house was an unimposing two up-two down building that suited the lawman well. Nate made for the boarding house, choosing a back route away from prying eyes and moving carefully to keep out of sight. He wanted no more questions and as little attention as possible. It had been a long night and he needed a bath and some rest before Isobel came to town. But it was not to be. He had just walked into Kim's boarding house when the door opened behind him and there stood the second deputy, Clem Ford, who had been up on the ridge with him the previous evening.

"Nate, saw you down the street, thought I'd find you here. You move mighty carefully. I like that in a man, especially one who might be hunted." The words hung in the air.

"Clem, I'm tired, hungry, and dirty, and I'm expecting company. Can this wait?"

"No, sir, not really."

Kim appeared in the doorway. "I hear you had quite a night," she said, raising an eyebrow.

"Yes, ma'am, I did."

"Well sit yourself down. I'll get you some breakfast and tea if that's what you'd like?"

"Ma'am, it certainly is. Clem, wait here a moment. At least let me wash away the smell of burnt powder and change my shirt." Without waiting for an answer, he moved to the stairs and made for his room. Ten minutes later he reappeared, changed and shaved. The smell of frying bacon was in the air and a pot of tea sat on the table with a jug of milk and some sugar.

Clem nodded and grinned: "You really drink that stuff?"

"I do. I prefer it when I can get it with milk. I'm English, after all," Nate said with a smile.

"English?"

"Yes. Long story, but my parents moved here from England when I was ten and I was brought up with a love of tea, fine cognac and a comfortable bed. Some habits die hard and none of those things are easily come by out west. Now tell me, what's so important?"

"Well, it's like this. The marshal's office is down to just one man. Lewis has a busted wing and he's only good for mindin' the jail, and I can't be in two places or more at once. So I was wonderin' if'n you'd help out 'til Andy and Tye get back into action again. I know the marshal asked you before to help out unofficially, and I wonder if you'd care to make it more official." His eyes leveled with Nate's.

"Look, I understand that you're in a fix, but there must be someone local who could and would step in," Nate replied. "It's not my town and I know nothing about being a lawman. I've never held a badge and I wouldn't know where to start. Also, I'll be off soon back to my ranch in Texas. It could be weeks before the marshal is up and about again."

"Not even for just a week?" Cal pleaded. "It would help control the bad element just knowing you were on board. You have already got quite a reputation, you know, and last night didn't hurt it none. Why, the way you threw down on those three gunnies was something to behold! We'd have been wolf bait if it hadn't been for you."

Nate shook his head. "I'd appreciate it if you would keep that to yourself. I don't want a reputation as a gunman."

Clem looked away, averting his eyes. "You might be a little late for that. Seems that the story's already out. That's what I meant when I said 'bout being hunted. The men behind the attempted raid on the mines will have heard by now, and I hear that some of 'em are lookin' for revenge. If you wore the badge it might well put 'em off."

Nate shook his head in disgust. "Or it might offer them a nice shiny target to aim at. Damn it, man, I wanted no part of this. I just saw a man about to be gunned down in cold blood at the saloon by a back-shooter, either you or more probably the marshal. I couldn't stand by and see it happen, and for that I get dragged into this sorry mess," Nate said, getting angrier each second. "I don't want a reputation as a gunman or a lawman. I'm a cattleman, a trail boss, and I came up here to see a girl. No more than that. A girl, I might add, who is coming into town today."

"Look ... I mean ... oh hell," Clem said, rising, "if you change your mind I'd really appreciate it."

Nate let out a long breath. "Alright, I understand. I'll think about it, but at the moment I won't do any more than I said. I'll look about me as I ride, like I promised Marshal Gorringe. Though I think that the only riding I'll be doing is heading south. Now, if you'll excuse me I need some shuteye."

"I'll be seeing you, Nate, and thanks again for helpin' us out last night. I sure appreciate it." Clem pushed his hat back on his head and left the boarding house.

Nate shook his head, staring into space, wondering where his life was going. As he forked up the last of the bacon and eggs and washed them down with tea, he leant back, pushing the chair onto two legs.

He heard Kim's voice. "There's a hot bath ready and I'll see you're not disturbed as you sleep."

"Thank you, ma'am, what would I do without you?" He smiled across at her. She snorted in mock disgust and left him to it.

Two hours later he woke from a sleep filled with dark dreams of gunfire and wild horses in the night. He sat up sweating, shaking his head to throw off the thoughts and images. He rose, washed his face and got dressed, stamping into his boots and slinging his gun belt around his waist, tying the pigging cord to his leg. Out of habit, he un-slipped the thong, slid the gun out and checked the loads before pinwheeling the Navy Colt and dropping it back into his holster. He repeated the process with the smaller Police Special, relaxed and then drew the right and left hand weapons. Smiling to himself, he replaced them in their holsters.

Nate hung the Stetson around his neck by the storm strap and tied his bandana in place. Thus satisfied, he made his way down the stairs to the dining room. He found that it was lunchtime and there was a hubbub of noise coming from the tables, most of which were occupied. All fell silent as he approached, then with the habit of western crowds, everyone appeared to mind their own business and carry on eating, with just a few nods of acknowledgment from those who he knew or had seen him around Langtonville.

Kim came up, bringing tea and milk. "Seems like you're a right popular fella."

"How so?"

"Well, after the deputy left, Mr. McKenzie came in from the mines. He's one of the three main owners, by the way, and after him two other miners came, along with a message from the sheriff who wants to see you later today."

The door opened, ringing the bell above, and in stepped a large, rough-looking man who seemed calloused all the way from his hands to a face that looked to be made of the same rock that he mined. His red beard was neatly trimmed and his coat open to reveal a revolver shoved into his waistband.

Coarse pants, patched at the knees, were tucked into working boots, and he hitched them up as he entered, then ran a huge hand through his dark red hair. He nodded at Kim who confirmed with a reciprocating nod in Nate's direction.

He marched up to Nate's table in a purposeful manner, all angles and sinew. "You'll be Nate Carlton?" he said in a Scottish burr.

"That I am," Nate answered noncommittally.

"Then it's a pleasure to meet you, laddie, for I hear we owe you a great debt for your actions last night. I'm Tam McKenzie, one of the three main owners of the Discovery Shaft." He held out a callused paw to shake Nate's hand.

Nate shook the tough hand, feeling the strength built by the dint of hard labor in the fierce grip. "How do you do? Please sit and join me."

"That's a refined accent ye've got. Are you English?"

"I am. My parents came over in '57 to South Carolina from London, when I was ten years old."

"Ach well, it cannae be helped, I suppose," he said with a rare twinkle in his blue eyes. "Grateful I am, and no mistake."

"Please, don't let me upset your niceties. I'm as happy to break bread with the Auld Enemy as any other."

"Ha! Ye'll do, laddie, ye'll do." McKenzie laughed, slapping the table and making some of the other customers jump. "I'm a straight talking Scot and apart from wanting to thank ye in person, I came to offer you a job, if you've a mind." McKenzie raised an eyebrow pausing to see how Nate would react.

"The answer is no, but out of curtesy I'll hear you out. Pray continue. Tea?"

"Damn it, ye're a nesh sassenach and no mistake. Nae, I'll have coffee if you please, Kim," he said turning to the landlady. "Well, ye'll hear me out, then. We have a pile of ore ready to be shipped from the mines, hence the attack on the blockhouse last night. Ye may have heard that Wells Fargo won't take it. Not enough guns to protect the shipment, and with only one man to ride shotgun, they'll not run the risk." He paused and watched as Nate stared at him over the brim of his teacup, from which he was contentedly sipping, giving nothing away by his expression. "Remind me not to play poker with you, laddie," McKenzie offered. "Now, as I was saying. No guards, no run. We tried with a dummy run, putting the word out that a shipment was being made. The stage got hit and the driver and guard were wounded, lucky to live. Now no one will do it without real protection, and that's where you come in. If you were riding shotgun, your gun skills and reputation would put the robbers off."

Nate's eyes hardened at this last comment. "Mr. McKenzie, as far as I am aware I have no reputation other than that of a man who helped out the marshal last night and got off a few lucky shots in the dark. And as I said to the deputy earlier today, I'm a cattleman and trail boss, not a lawman or a shotgun guard."

"Och, get off your high horse, laddie. I meant no offence, yet ye cannae deny that you brought a herd through, facing down Brannigan's herd cutters and besting Randall and his crew in Dodge last year. Aye, and even now I hear the story of three gunslingers who are no longer with us who tried to cut your herd a few days ago. Ye're not a man to back water, and your skill—whether sought or not—brings with it the reputation of man not to be crossed or pushed around."

Nate snorted in disgust, ignoring the praise. "Why not send a group of miners as outriders with the stagecoach? Give them each a rifle. The mines seem big enough to raise an armed guard to ride with the coach. It would certainly put off a gang of holdup men if the odds were against them," Nate reasoned.

"Yes and no. We've thought of that, but these are miners. They may have fought in the war and all, but they're no gunmen, sitting in the open waiting for an ambush. They wouldn't know how to defend the coach and they'd probably scatter out in the open, leaving it open to attack, tough as they may be. No, it needs someone to coordinate and plan things, someone who knows how a gunfight works and who to take down in the event of an ambush. Someone who can read the land and the route to Denver with the assay office there, along with a strong bank and a railroad."

"Why, that's nigh on a hundred and fifty miles," Nate said. "That would be three days' travel at least, even with stage changes."

"That's exactly my point. Too far for outriders to cover it all the way and be safe."

"Like I said before, Mr. McKenzie, the answer is no to this, and no to being a lawman. Yet I am flattered to think that you consider me worthy of your trust."

"Well think on it, laddie, think on it. Dinnae say no just yet. I'll pay you a hundred and fifty dollars a day to see the stage safely to Denver," he said with raised eyebrows and a gleam in his eyes. "And believe me that hurts a Scot to lay out such funds to an Englishman."

"McKenzie, you're a wily old devil!" Nate replied. "But the answer is still no."

"Och, I'll be back, laddie, I'll be back." The Scot drained the dregs from his coffee cup, rose, shook Nate's hand and left as quickly as he had entered, a purposeful look upon his face.

Nate sat there staring into space, considering all that he had heard. It was in his mind to consider a plan; he couldn't help himself. He had studied tactics in the war, listening carefully and respecting the more experienced leaders, of whom he knew there were many on both sides. He'd seen battles and skirmishes won and lost on good or bad planning and was able to sense whether a plan of action was good or not before it happened. Despite himself, he saw a way of making it work. Or at least he thought he did.

Maybe I'm just a bad leader who thinks he's good. He smiled to himself. *Time to get myself back home to Texas.*

His next thoughts were far from gunfights and stage holdups, for as he walked along the street upon leaving the boarding house he spotted a smart surrey pulled up in front of the general store harnessed to two fine matched greys. *Nice horses*, he mused, and it didn't take him long to work out who the surrey belonged to. As if to confirm his thoughts, he saw three more quality mounts by its side, each bearing the brand of the Circle Hart ranch. Nate smiled with pleasure for the first time in two days' as he stepped into the cool gloom of the store. He heard her before he saw her, asking her father for a new dress just in from the east. Nate walked up into her line of sight.

"Nate! Good morning, I was hoping I might see you in town," she said.

"Morning, Miss Isobel, it's lovely to see you. You too, Mr. Hart," he replied, nodding politely and tipping his hat. Her father frowned in displeasure. Not giving him the chance to intercede, Nate dived in. "I was wondering if you'd do me the honor of sharing a cup of coffee with me?"

"I'd be delighted, Mr. Carlton, although I thought you English drank tea." She presented him a grin. "I'll see you later, Papa, don't forget that dress now." She gave her father a little wave and linked her arm into Nate's before her father could object or her mother could appear from the other side of the store, where she was talking to some townswomen whose husbands were on the town council. "Come, let's make ourselves scarce," she urged in a conspiratorial whisper. "Before Mama can get her claws into you."

The pair swept out onto the street and found a quiet café a few doors down. With coffee and bear sign ordered they sat and became absorbed in conversation, with Isobel hardly pausing for breath between sips of coffee. She finally stopped to savor the bear sign.

"Oh my, these are good," she exclaimed.

"They certainly are, but not as good as the company," he flattered her.

"Do you know, I've missed good manners and charming company out here," Isobel said. "All I get are rough cowboys or new gunmen for company. It's so tiresome. The townswomen are old, and their daughters seem to be indifferent to any new company or anything the least bit adventurous. It's lonely out here, I find. Not like back home, where I had a good circle of friends, and dances and parties to go to. All Papa talks about is business and cattle, with private meetings all the time.

"Listen to me, I'm prattling on and haven't had the manners to ask about you." She reached a hand across to cover his in a movement of innocent affection, yet the heat of the touch seemed to inflame Nate.

"I guess it can be tough out here for a woman, especially someone who's just in from the east," he replied. "A completely different way of life. Usually there'd be dances each month and a social circle among the rancher's daughters mixing in with the townswomen and the young bloods. I mean, it won't compare to Boston society, but it would be a social life and chance to mix with people your own age."

"Maybe I should organize something, get some invitations out. Mama seems to have ingratiated herself with all the local ladies of importance," she declared wickedly. "But tell me, what you've been doing? I heard that you brought your second herd in and are getting a good reputation as a trail boss."

Nate found he enjoyed her company and told her about his ideas for syndicated drives, about his ranch in Texas and what his plans for the future were. Then he explained about the marshal getting shot and his part in the proceedings, which he played down significantly. They talked for longer over their second cup of coffee until Mrs. Hart entered the coffee shop and strode over to their table, the eyes of all the other customers upon her.

Nate rose politely and nodded to her. "Mrs. Hart, good morning, ma'am," he said.

"It is now afternoon," she responded tersely. "Isobel, come, I need you to choose some clothes."

"Mother we haven't finished coffee yet, won't you join us?" Isobel answered firmly, refusing to be bullied by her overbearing mother. Nate admired her spirit, but it was not enough.

"Isobel, I will not have you associating with killers," she said dramatically. "This man was involved in a gunfight yesterday evening, I hear, and killed some men both in town and at the mines. I've seen him kill before and now he's doing it again."

The eyes of all the customers in the café turned on Nate, and for a moment Isobel looked a little shocked. She recovered quickly. "But, mother, Nate explained that he was helping the marshal—"

"Not another word. Come with me now."

Despite her protests she allowed her mother to take her arm and lead her from the table, Nate listening her mother berating her for associating with murderers and cowboys as they left.

He sat down, embarrassed, shaking his head.

From a nearby table one of a group of miners said: "Don't you pay her no never mind, son. She's eastern and we're grateful for your help last night. If'n it weren't for you we'd have lost our ore, and no mistake. We'd admire to buy you a cup of coffee or something a mite stronger at the saloon, the sun bein' up and high in the sky."

Nate was about to refuse, then he thought *what the hell*

and accepted their offer. The group headed for the Northern Star where they settled at a quiet table by the rear wall with their drinks before them.

The leader, Si Holder, carried the conversation, talking about transporting the ore. "See, we've been thinkin' of ways to transport it, and we figure that you might be the answer."

Nate offered him a wintry smile. "The boss put you up to this?" he asked. "Nice try, boys, but the answer's no. I already had a conversation with McKenzie this very morning. I'm a cattleman, not a stagecoach shotgun rider."

"Yea, but you have the know-how and the skill," Si continued stubbornly.

"Well, I'm not convinced about that, but if you want a gunman, hire one, there are plenty around. Try the Circle Hart, there sure seem to be a lot of them hanging around there," Nate suggested.

Si snorted in disgust. "Ha, fat lot of good they'd do, working for that Hart fella. We hear he's as crooked as they come and out to get mines, land and cattle along with part of the town. You'll pardon my bluntness if you're after courtin' his daughter, but word gets around, you know."

This was a revelation to Nate. He did not know that Hart's reach had grown so far, yet he could still not reconcile Isobel's father with that role. Despite the fact that he was an overbearing, pompous bully, it just seemed too much of a stretch.

"Also," Si continued, "we don't know how to hire gunmen, and even if we did, we don't know to trust 'em. Might just be working for the other side as much as for us. A gunny is just a paid hand and he'll always foller the money, whoever is paying. Trust, a good reputation, and decency, son, now they are much rarer qualities, and you got 'em. Now, with the marshal and one deputy out it's all going to blow wide open. There'll be hell to pay, and you know it. Town's gonna blow up like a powder keg with a short fuse lit," he declared, his voice rising, causing some stares from within the saloon.

A swish of skirts and the smell of perfume heralded Candy's presence. Looking as glamorous as ever, she placed a gentle but somehow proprietorial hand upon Nate's shoulder, causing him to look upward into her beautiful face. Her eyes were sharp and hidden in their depths was something that Nate could not fathom as he looked at her. She wagged an admonishing finger at Si Holder. "Now just you listen here, you old goat," she said. "Don't you go frightening all my customers with your tales of doom, gloom and terror. I declare you'll put me out of business." Her smile robbed the words of any sting.

"Sorry, Candy, but we're just about at our wits' end, what with the raid on the mine and everythin'. We're just trying to persuade Nate here to ride shotgun on the stage and keep a load safe for us."

"Are you minded to help these men?" she asked Nate, her tone more serious.

"No, ma'am, I am not. I'm a cattleman as I keep telling these chaps. I'm not a gun for hire."

"I'm right pleased to hear it. Sounds like a stacked deck whichever way you look at it," she offered, giving his shoulder a gentle, almost imperceptible squeeze.

"See, boys? Listen to the lady," Nate joked.

"Waal, just you give it some thought, young fella. We need you." The four miners got up, bade Candy good day, and left for their afternoon's work at the mine.

"Just you take care, Nate. I'd hate to see you caught up in all this local trouble." Candy stared into his eyes.

"Yes, ma'am. I have no intention of being—" he began.

"But there might be one thing more dangerous than looking after gold and silver. Like I told you last night, my name is Candy, and calling me ma'am makes me feel like my life's done," she admonished him.

"Sure, Candy." Nate smiled at her. "Now I have to go about some business. I'll see you later, and I'll get some fresh coffee if you don't have tea." He rose and tipped his hat and headed for the door. As he pushed through the doors he found a young boy of about ten waiting for him outside the saloon.

"Mister, are you Nate Carlton?"

"Yes I am, son. How may I help you."

"Here." He offered a folded note. "Lady asked me to give you this."

"Thank you." He fished into his vest pocket, flipped the young boy a coin and opened the letter. It was from Isobel, and she asked that he meet her at nine o'clock tomorrow morning by the two oak trees at the fork in the road at the head of their ranch.

Nate smiled. His spirits were raised by the thought that all was not lost, and he promised himself that he'd be there.

Chapter Nine

Nate set out early the following day to keep his appointment with Isobel. There had been more shootings in the town the night before, with two men killed in gunfights and arguments that had spewed out on to the streets with brawls and knife fights. He had stayed well clear, but he had received a note from the marshal asking to see him later today when he returned from his ride. He mentally agreed to the invitation but had already decided what his answer would be.

He remembered the trail easily and followed it to the two oak trees that marked the fork in the road where he had ridden days earlier. He spotted Isobel in the distance, dismounted and sitting under one of the oaks in the shade of the early morning sun, her horse cropping grass with the reins over a low branch. The animal stopped at the sound of Buck's hooves on the trail and looked up, ears pricked. The shaded figure rose, walking out into the full sun, raising a hand to shade her eyes as she looked up the trail. Seeing him she waved. Nate loped up the rise and stopped easily. He saw that she had on a white blouse, a divided grey skirt and black cowboy boots. A grey Stetson was pushed back off her head and she looked to his eyes a perfect picture.

He smiled at her. "Well, you sure are a sight for sore eyes first thing in the morning."

"Oh, Nate, I'm so glad you made it," she said, walking up as he dismounted. "I wondered if you would come after the way my mother spoke to you yesterday, for which I must apologize."

"There's no need, Isobel. Mothers are like that. She's just looking after your best interests," he said generously.

"I think she is full of schemes and aspirations for me. Papa's banker, Moises Letterman, has a nephew who is coming out to visit soon and there is already pressure there. Mama is forever telling me what a nice young man he is, and how good his prospects are." She mimicked her mother's voice and manner perfectly. "But if he is anything like his uncle, I think I'd rather shoot myself."

This made Nate laugh and it broke the tension between them. "Shall we ride? It's still quite cool and I'd like to see more of the country, which can only be improved by the company I'm in," Nate said smoothly.

She gave him an encouraging smile, gathered up her horse's reins and mounted in a fluid motion. Nate followed her example, and they were soon loping across fine green grassland where cattle grazed at peace with the world. Again, Nate was surprised at how many creeks and streams crossed the land, offering life-giving water to the lush vegetation.

They slowed the horses to a walk, and the conversation drifted between them. A couple of times Nate looked around, getting a feeling that they were not alone, yet no one seemed in evidence, and he didn't want to ruin the moment. They rode down a slight incline to a spot where the stream widened into a small pond, across which were a series of small rocks forming stepping stones to the other side. Two swaying willows and a clump of aspens grew here, offering welcome shade as the heat of the day was slowly building. Their conversation continued as they dismounted and sat by the pond, easy in each other's company.

Under the shade of the willows, Nate reached up to push aside a stray strand of her Isobel's hair and kissed her gently on the lips. She responded in kind and slipped into his arms, seeking an embrace. They broke to breathe and smiled at each other, happy and contented.

Then the moment changed. Nate looked around again suspiciously, wondering if he'd seen the flash of a reflection.

"What's the matter? Is everything all right?" Isobel asked following his gaze.

"Sure, just a feeling that someone was watching us." He tried to laugh the moment off. "Guess I've been riding too many dark trails."

She frowned, the spell broken. "Is what Mama said about killing those men true? She made you sound like a desperado."

Nate let out a sigh. "I helped the sheriff, like I told you, but he asked me to, and it was a spur of the moment thing. If I hadn't, he and I would probably be dead now. Out here it's not like the east, where you can call a constable and have the law solve all your problems."

"I understand, but she mentioned that time on the boat

where you also shot and killed a man. It just seems so brutal and unnecessary, though I'm trying to understand this new wild world that we're now living in."

For once Nate was lost for words. She was describing the very things that disturbed him about the way his life was evolving, and wanted to be no more a part of it than was absolutely necessary. "Well," he began, "the thing is, out here guns are tools, like a shovel or a hoe. A necessary tool, no more no less. And it's not the tools, it's who uses them and how they are used that matters. All I can say is that I've never provoked a fight or drawn first on a man who has not thrown down on me, or who meant to kill me or my friend like what happened on the riverboat."

Her blue eyes searched his intently. "OK. I'll try to understand, and I won't say any more about it." With that she twisted round to lay her head in his lap. She plucked a long ear of grass and began to tease him, tickling his nose with it. The moment had passed, yet the memory of it still hung in the air between them.

An hour later, they parted at the fork with the oak trees and said goodbye, promising to meet in town in three days' time when the Harts came to town for their regular Saturday visit.

He waved as he crested the rise, and once out of sight he pushed Buck into a fast lope, keen to be away and clear his head. On impulse he skirted around to the box canyon where he had practiced before and decided that he would burn some powder with a little practice.

Ground hitching Buck in the shade within reach of some coarse grass, he set up some sticks on the large log he had used before. He tied off the cord to his leg, slipped off the thong and began drawing first his left and then his right gun. Satisfied after half an hour of various positions and moves, he started firing at the targets. They exploded in a shower of splinters, each shot finding its mark.

He carried a spare cylinder on his belt in a loop pocket, and shutting his eyes he flicked open the barrel and fed in the new cylinder by feel before closing up the mechanism and firing once more. He then did a double Border Shift as fast as he could, flicking the Navy to his left hand and drawing the Police Special with blinding speed, emptying the small caliber weapon into a closer target. It did not have the range of the longer barreled gun and needed sighting for longer distance work to make it really accurate. But that was not its job. It was a backup weapon.

When he'd emptied his guns, he walked back to his horse and reloaded again. Twice more he repeated the actions until he was happy with speed and accuracy. He also tried his newly acquired cavalry twist draw, which was now nearly as fast as his standard right hand draw.

Then he tried some trick shots, including the Road Agent's Spin, dropping and firing from different positions, turning and drawing as he had for Billy Jo and Frank on the trail that seemed a lifetime ago. He burned more powder and did a final target shoot, throwing three cones in the air, dropping his hand in a reflex action to blast each one as they fell to earth. The Navy was now empty. Nate started to walk towards Buck, who stood patiently, then he saw the horse's head fly up, ears pricked and nostrils flared.

"Mister, that's your six and you're outta luck and

bullets." A voice floated across from a boulder at the entrance to the canyon. The man had clearly sneaked up in all the noise, and not even Buck had heard him approach until it was too late.

Nate stopped dead, turning slowly.

"Easy does it, Mister Nate Carlton. This Henry won't miss. I don't care how fast you are, and like I said, I counted six and you're empty."

Nate saw Chas Goodman, the hardcase from the Circle Hart, and another gun-toting tough from the ranch.

"You?"

"Yeah, me. Mr. Hart doesn't like saddle tramps sparkin' his daughter and sent us out here to dissuade you- permanently!" Goodman sneered. "So, mister gunman, drop your gun belt and we'll send you on your way."

Nate made to untie the leg thong on his leg, and then slowly reached for the belt buckle with his right hand. He knew that once disarmed they would cripple or kill him. They were vicious sadistic killers, with no morals or scruples. They were too far away for instinctive shooting using the Police Special. Its short barrel would be inaccurate, especially against two men. His own rifle lay in its scabbard on Buck and his Navy was empty. He needed an edge, and he didn't have one. His mind raced, looking for an opening.

Then he got a break. A report sounded from the top of the mesa overlooking the canyon, and a puff of dirt spurted up at Goodman's feet.

Nate didn't hesitate. He dived sideways to get what cover he could, drawing the smaller Colt as he did so. His movement ended in a forward roll behind a small outcrop of rocks that were barely big enough to conceal him. Yet the distraction had been enough, and more shots pinged and ricocheted around the two gunmen, who dived for cover and moved back out of the draw, all thoughts of shooting Nate forgotten. Seeking a reprieve, they ran to where their horses were standing and using them as cover they slapped them into a run, doing a Pony Express mount by bouncing their feet off the ground to land in the saddle. They swiftly galloped away out of range.

Nate rose, shading his eyes against the sun, trying to see who his savior was and beckoning Buck over to him, where his own Spencer lay attached to his saddle. Once it was in his grasp he felt happier, levering a shell into the breech and cocking the hammer back in case the two regained their nerve and came back.

"You alright, Nate?" a voice shouted from the top of the mesa. Nate recognized it as Linus Farnham's.

A few minutes later Linus appeared around the entrance to the draw, a big grin on his face. "Never figured the day I'd be able help you out in a gunfight," he said.

"I'm delighted that you came along. I thought my goose was cooked for certain, and I'm very grateful."

"Glad to be of service. I was rounding up strays in the next valley like last time, heard the shooting and thought I'd come and see how it was done. Thought it'd be you. Mighty glad I did, those fellas seemed set on a killing. Too far for accurate shooting so thought I'd scare 'em off and give you a break."

"Well, you certainly did that, and any time you're in

trouble, just shout and I'll be there." Nate nodded, tipping his hat.

"I'll remember that," he said. "Now come on back and have some coffee. The wife's been bakin', so it won't be so bad."

Chapter Ten

The coffee, doughnuts and company had been good at the Farnham ranch and with the ease of such a quiet environment, Nate, with Laura's permission, had stripped and cleaned his guns, laying them out on an old cloth covering the table.

She had watched Nate treat the weapons almost reverently, knowing that these were more than just tools to Nate, but an extension of him and the difference between life and death. This contrasted so deeply with the polite young man before her that it gave Laura a greater curiosity, wondering at his background and asking questions that she probably shouldn't have, giving Nate pause for thought as well.

Now rested and more relaxed after his brush with fate, he entered town quietly off one of the side trails that took him directly to Kim's boarding house. After stopping there for lunch he moved on to the livery stable, unsaddling his horse and then went to the marshal's house as he had promised.

He found the lawman more comfortable, yet still a grey pallor showed under his tan, with lines etched around his eyes, both of worry and pain. His voice, when he spoke, was stronger and less croaky. Nurse Mallory was fussing over him and admonished that he spend no more than ten minutes as the marshal was still very weak.

"Good to see you, son. I hear you've been pestered high and low by all comers." He smiled at Nate.

"That I have, and seems I'm mighty unpopular all round. I was setup by a couple of Hart's gunnies today, damn nearly had me if it hadn't been for Farnham turning up and saving my bacon. I was damn lucky."

"How so?" At which Nate explained what had happened.

"You still sweet on that girl, then?"

Nate gave a shy smile. "Well, it's got to the point that I'm just being stubborn. Her mother doesn't like me and her father sent a couple of gunman to see me off or worse. I don't like being told not to do something, when I've every right to do it. So even if she wasn't pretty and good company I'd still carry. But on that note, Clem has a pretty low opinion of her father, anything else I should know or just what you have told me already?"

"Well, that sort of ties in with what I wanted to see you about. We had two more killings last night and with only Clem around, there will be many more deaths. Everyone is aware of this, now that all know the gold and silver can't be shipped.

"The miners are all hold up with them all running on credit for supplies and such like. It's all getting tight. The mines are plum pickings, everyone wants some of it; the land is in play for cattle and everyone being pushed around. Even the town's changing with stores being bought up by God knows who," he finished weakly, reaching for a glass of water.

"You know that is the one thing that puzzles me. This is a rough crowd and no mistake. The way I have heard of this happening before in strike towns, even before the war, the bad element would move in, along with sharks, gamblers, card sharp artists, killers, opportunists and whoever. Included in that scum of humanity would be claim jumpers; men who follow the strikes, kill or intimidate and get hold of the claims. Force their way in. Yet this seems all intact. How so? You can't tell me everyone is loyal and there are no rats up at the mines with just one big happy family?" he asked.

"No, and that's a good question. It comes down to McKenzie, he's a shrewd man and knows the ropes. In a nutshell it works like this: every man jack of them who make a claim sign off one share to the main holding company. Just a dollar share, but for any transfer of mining rights to any claim. It has by law to get the acceptance of the company. It also needs the current owner to be alive and present at the signing. If not, it reverts to the company and they buy it giving the value to the dependents of the deceased. Well, that's the gist of it, anyway. Mighty good idea but as McKenzie would say himself he's a *mighty cannee scotchman!*" The marshal gave a terrible impersonation of McKenzie's accent.

"It's Scotsman, scotch is the drink," Nate corrected with a grin robbing his words of the sting. "But you've got that right, a clever move."

"Well, whatever. The point is, as far as it goes, the mine is secure for now, but with little law it won't last long. We were lucky last time, thanks to you. Which brings me back to the reason I wanted to see you. I know Clem asked you but would you just see your way clear to wearing a badge for a few days until Lewis is back. He says he can't move his shoulder, let alone fire a gun and he's hopeless with his left hand.

"I know it's a lot to ask and you have no interest, but I have to try. It's my town and I feel responsible."

Nate shook his head. "Marshal, I'm no lawman, as I said to Clem and to McKenzie about riding shotgun. Already Isobel thinks I'm halfway to being a gunman and a killer, just because I intervened and helped you before. I'm seeing Isobel on Saturday and we'll see how it goes then. I'm probably going to head back to my ranch in Texas. I'm sorry, but there it is."

Marshal Gorringe looked sad and dismayed, laying back after his impassioned plea, sinking back into the pillows. "Alright, but I had to try. I appreciate all you did for me that night. But just give it some thought, that's all I ask."

At which point Nurse Mallory opened the door and strode in. "Time for you to leave, mister Carlton! You have tired my patient enough," she commanded.

Nate apologized and bid goodbye to the marshal and left, his thoughts turning in his head. He was torn: he did not want the job or the responsibilities that came with it, not to mention the reputation that would follow. He had feelings for Isobel that were growing, yet equally he did not know where that was leading as there were many impediments to furthering any relationship, not least of which her parents.

Which led to another question in his mind, why send men after him to frighten him off or worse, possibly kill him? Why not just tell him straight? Hell, he thought with an inward smile, her mother was more frightening than Chas Goodman the gunny from the Circle Hart! Also was Hart really behind the landgrab and was it tied into the mine raids, which were clearly well coordinated and linked, if only by virtue of the setup with Shaun McCrae.

It was all very complicated and he was only seeing part of the puzzle. So much for not getting involved, yet his mind worked that way. His father had taught him to always seek the truth and look after the weak. Nate shook his head as though distancing himself from his thoughts, heading back to the boarding house.

Wanting a quiet night, he decided to leave town and camp in the prairie somewhere where it was unobtrusive so he could think. He told Kim, who asked if her beds were lumpy. He told her no, but just needed time alone in the silence of what promised to be a warm, starlit night. She understood instinctively and made some bear sign for him, cooked chicken and offered a small sealed tin of fresh milk. "For your tea or coffee, as you please."

He fetched Patch from the livery, alternating his rides and left town whilst it was still light, feeling eyes upon him as he did so. He went south for two miles then headed up an old game trail, barely wide enough for his horse as he pushed through thick brush and thickets of aspen, rocky mountain juniper and gambel oak. At times it was so thick he lost the trail and had to meander, left and right, dismounting and cutting branches with his clasp knife. This way he knew he was not followed.

The trail rose steeply coming out onto an escarpment of sandstone, offering a panoramic view of the basin. In the fading light from this vantage point he dismounted so as not to outline himself against the skyline, then squatted low back from the edge: he could make out the mines, the town and dotted beacons of light indicating farms, homesteads and ranches. The Circle Hart was not within sight, being over a ridge to the west. It was a lovely valley he reflected and too good for which fate had decided was its future.

He made a camp back in a copse, finding dry wood that produced little smoke and under some cottonwoods it was further filtered, so no outward sign was showing to anyone unless right on top of his camp. He hobbled Patch in some lush grass and found a small trickle of water running down the sandstone rock face, just at an entrance to a small cave. Over a long period of time it had eroded a small natural basin within the sandstone, almost a foot deep, acting as a natural water trough. After heating water and making coffee, he put the fire out and moved back into the woods, making a new camp in the cave, sheltered and secure. Tomorrow would be a new day and it would all seem different in the morning. He lay back on his suggan, head resting on his saddle, listening to the sounds of the night as he drifted off into sleep with thoughts of Isobel on his mind.

He awoke from a dreamless sleep hours later, unaware of the time. Something had awoken him. A man on the trail is rarely if ever, deeply asleep, one small part of him is always alert to the sounds and changes of the environment around him. Nate pulled up his body, ears questing the night, all senses alert. Nothing was caught on the breeze so he looked over to Patch who was quiet with no signs of agitation. Something had disturbed his sleep and that worried him. Then he heard it. Gunfire coming from the town, multiple shots fired into the night, echoing across the valley. Then the deafening silence that always comes after violence.

Nate pulled out his pocket watch from his calfskin vest, he flicked open the spring lid protecting the face. It had been a present from his father, who gave it to him just before he went off to war and was his most treasured possession. By the dim light he read just before one o'clock in the morning. Just some yahoos, hooraying the town he surmised. He pushed the lid closed, pulled his hat down and tried to go back to sleep. From then on he slept fitfully and was awake with the dawn, senses immediately alert. Something was nagging at his subconscious and he did not like it.

He fried up some bacon and dropped a couple of eggs into the fat watching them bubble as the whites changed color, his thoughts far away wondering what the shooting was about last night. He still had an uneasy feeling.

With breakfast eaten, he put in an hour's practice with his pistols, thinking about how he was caught unawares before and vowed to get another handgun to keep as a spare for when he was practicing alone. One he could lodge in his belt, perhaps with the new metallic cartridges he'd heard about. Maybe a Remington Beals would suit, he considered.

He cleared his camp, leaving a pile of dry wood at the back of the cave as was ranch country practice for any other traveler along the road. Nate tacked up Patch and rode down a different trail to the east of the town, bringing him down behind the hills of the mining camp.

The trail see-sawed down steeply from the mesa, following the line of a narrow stream, that broke to a small waterfall dropping about thirty feet to a pool below. Unfortunately, he saw that the track, only used by game, seemed to taper off stopping at the lip of the fall. It was narrow here and he would have to edge around and go back up. Then as Nate guided Patch, the Appaloosa nudged forward thinking that Nate wanted him to pass by a crop of hazel that had sprouted out of the rock. Patch grabbed a mouthful and pushed inwards, the juicy young shoots protruding from his mouth as he munched around the copper sweet iron bit. With the parting of the bush, a small trail was suddenly evident and Nate was nearly unseated as Patch barged through the narrow gap. Once past, the trail opened out again covered above by a canopy of hazel that formed a gallery of speckled light for about fifty feet, dropping gently downwards.

At the bottom he stopped and twisting in the saddle looked back: "Well, I'll be damned," he muttered, "clever horse." Patting the stallion's neck, he pushed on finding an established trail between two sandstone pillars, standing like watchmen guarding the way. Once here, as he had suspected, he was now on the eastern side of the hills where the mining was taking place, although such was the height of his position, neither sight nor sound of the works was could be heard.

He rode easily enjoying the day and the peace and quiet,

looking down at the trail constantly, yet alert. This was still Cheyenne country and he did not want to be taken unawares. The trail widened, skirting the base of the hills and was heavily wooded, offering little opportunity to see more than a few feet ahead, so dense were the trees. Then it broke off to the right, heading deep into the footings. Out of curiosity Nate followed the fork. Like most westerners he was always interested in the land and where things led, forming mental maps in his head.

Pine and aspen had been felled here to form a clearing and two new log chutes were fed by a stream that had been dammed to a greater pressure with a sluice gate. Two openings forming the heads of shafts had been started into the side of the hillside disappearing into darkness. Nate was instantly curious wondering if McKenzie and the others knew this was here. He dismounted and looked closely at the sign upon the dried mud. There were many tracks, some of them recent and evidence of recent workings. *This is odd,* he thought, *wonder who has been working these shafts?* Then, probing around he saw two small wooden shacks had been constructed deep into the woodland and hidden from view. Each had a hasp securely locked with a padlock, which was frustrating, yet Nate had no intention of anyone knowing that he had been there.

His curiosity peaked more than ever. Nate remounted and rode on back to the trail, skirting the hill line to the north. He saw a cutting between two knolls and took this, riding over the top of the hill line and down again to arrive a couple of hours later in the western valley, close to the mine workings. He wanted no part of them or to be pestered by

McKenzie and Si Holder, so rode on by with sufficient distance to not be easily recognized, if indeed he was seen at all.

It had indeed been an interesting ride and set his curious mind down paths that he wished not to travel.

Chapter Eleven

His day of peace was soon disturbed as he entered the town from the east. It was curiously quiet, with a subdued atmosphere pervading the air, or maybe it was just his imagination.

He rode up the end of Main Street to the first buildings and stopped outside Kim's boarding house not believing what he was seeing. Two windows were smashed with temporary boardings up on them, and there were bullet holes in the woodwork, including the door and frame. Luckily, they had been stoutly built and appeared to have stopped the rounds from entering. He shook his head not believing the evidence of his eyes. Dismounting, he hurriedly looped the reins over the hitching rail and ran up the steps into the house.

"Kim, ma'am? You there?" he called. She appeared as the chimes of the doorbell faded, a shotgun in her hands, face streaked with dirt and the smell of smoke in the air.

"Oh, Nate it's you!" she exclaimed, shaking and lowering the shotgun. Ying hovered at the doorway behind her, a meat cleaver in his hand ready to throw it. At seeing Nate he too relaxed and disappeared behind the door, muttering to himself in Chinese.

Nate strode forward to hold her by the shoulders, then took her into his arms as she broke down sobbing. "It's alright," he said soothingly, remembering his mother doing the same when he told her he was going off to war. "Tell me what happened."

"They came last night, trouble been brewin all evening, fights and gunfire. Then there was a brawl at the Barrel saloon, it drew a crowd and went onto the street with rowdies firing their six guns into the air. Deputy Clem came down, to break it up, tried to close the place down. Oh, it was terrible, Nate, the worst yet." Here she paused, shaking her head, wiping tears from her eyes. Collecting herself she continued. "They seemed to surround him forming a ring, he didn't know which way to turn. Then the fighting seemed to stop. McCrae stepped forward, asking what the deputy was going to do. Told him he was goin' to close him down, that he'd had enough of his saloon and all the killings and robberies. McCrae laughed at him, and then out of nowhere a shot was fired at his feet and a cry of 'watch out, marshal he has gun'! Clem had a rifle and leveled it at where the shot came from, then another shot came from the other side. I saw it all from my window. Then it was chaos with a volley of shots from all around the ring. When the shootin' stopped the deputy lay dead in the street, all shot up." She clamped her eyes shut as if to blot out the vision that was irrevocably stamped upon her mind. "The mayor came down with two council members then, and the doctor, but it was too late. He was a brave man who died doing his duty."

Nate let her talk, but wanting to know about this place.

"And here?" he asked.

"Oh, after the body was taken away, with the mayor and the others backing up the street behind a shotgun and a rifle, it started again. A group came this way shoutin' that there was one more lawman they had to get, meaning you, Nate. They had bandanas over their faces, couldn't see who it was. But they came as a mob, demanding that you be sent out so they could deal with anyone who had sided with the marshal. They shot out my windows, fired at the door and someone threw an oil lamp through. Ying was quick, bless him, and fearless. Got a wet table cloth and doused the fire before it could get started. I came to the door with my shotgun and said that you had left town.

"I was so scared, thought they were going to burn me out. Then some neighbors came out, including Milly and her husband from next door, stood out front and gave them what for. One said that he'd not make war on women and after that the group sort of broke up and drifted. It was awful. Just awful." She shuddered and Nate let her sit down easing her into a chair. "After my husband died of cholera, I came west to find a new life, be at ease and enjoy my later years, get away from pain and sufferin'. Looks like it's not meant to be."

"Ma'am you have my word. You'll have a peaceful life

here again. You've suffered because of me. I will not have it."
He felt a cold anger burning in him, that he had deserted
Clem Ford who now lay dead and this poor woman terrorized because they wanted him. Well, they were going to get
him, but not as they imagined.

"No, Nate, no. You're a young man with a future ahead
of you. Leave, go away, I'll be fine. They're brutal killers who
will stop at nothin'."

Nate smiled down at her. "Yes, ma'am. But what I'd like
now is a cup of coffee and some bear sign if you have any, all
this talking has made me hungry."

The complete about face in Nate's demeanor from
serious to food and coffee made Kim laugh and shake her
head for a moment, her troubles forgotten. But once she rose
and headed for the kitchen, Nate's face hardened into a mask
of anger as he planned what he intended to do. It became a
campaign of war to him now, bringing all his experience to
bear, hearing in his head the advice of senior officers, his
father and even dear Sam, and by God he wished that he was
here now at his side. A picture was beginning to form in his
mind.

The whole scenario was far more complex than anyone
imagined and a good mind was behind all this; he was
convinced that it wasn't just isolated incidents of a town out
of control exploding by virtue of gold and silver strikes. Too
much interconnected. Then he thought it was still early and
his horse was out at the front easily identifiable. "Kim," he
called out, "have you got any kind of stall around the back,
out of sight?"

"Yes," she said appearing in the doorway. "I keep Matilda, my old mule there. Why?"

"I just need to get Patch off the street before anyone sees him and want him out of sight for a short while."

"Sure, help yourself, go in by the side alley. There's a spare stall and some hay there, fork him some out and give him some corn to if'n you've a mind," she said easily.

With this done, Nate returned via the back door having seen no one on the street at this early hour. With doughnuts and coffee consumed, he slipped out of the back door again, along the side streets making for the marshal's house.

He knocked and found Nurse Mallory sitting in a rocking chair dozing, a shawl around her shoulders and a huge Colt Dragoon lying in her hand on her lap. At his knock she jumped raising the gun as though she knew what it was for, the hammer already cocked. Nate stopped dead raising his hands. "Ma'am, it's only me and that canon will put a hole in me bigger than anything you can fix, so I would really appreciate it if you pointed it away from me."

She blinked twice and came back to reality. "I'm so sorry. It has been one heck of a night." At which she eased the hammer down as Nate breathed a sigh of relief. "They came here last night, tried the door and I showed them my pistol and told them I'd blow their fool heads off if they came inside."

Nate had to laugh at this doughty woman. "Now, ma'am, where did you get that piece of artillery? It certainly would have a way of dissuading men. You get shot with a Colt Dragoon anywhere and there won't be much left of you," he joked, knowing she must be strong, the gun weighed all of four pounds and kicked like a Missouri mule, spewing a deadly .44 lead ball that splattered anything in its path.

"It was my father's gun. He carried it until the day he died and it took the life of the man who killed him. Though I'm not proud of the fact." Her eyes dropped. "That's why I took up nursing to save lives, not take them." A strained silence filled the parlor. The frontier was tough and it bred tough people, fighters in a land where there was little or no law. She would do to ride the river with, Nate decided.

"Is the marshal upstairs, I need to see him?"

"He is, but go easy on him, if you know what I mean?"

Nate nodded and started to climb the stair, hearing an occasional thump as he did. Puzzled, he carried on. He knocked and was beckoned in by a curt command. Marshal Gorringe was stood up leaning on a wooden crutch, an Army Colt in his hand pointed at the door. "Nate! It's you, we thought you were dead or long gone."

"Marshal, seems like it's the day for pointing guns at me. That'll be the third today," Nate said steadily.

"I'm sorry and more than a little upset and angry. Did you hear what happened to Clem last night? All because I'm busted up and useless."

"I heard and I'm just as sad as you. He was a good man. I also saw what they did to Kim's place looking for me. Seems that they wanted to clear the board and have free rein. I don't like being pushed and for what it's worth, I feel guilty about Clem. If I had been here last night he might still be alive."

"Doubt it, they'd have gone for you too and you'd be

lying in a coffin now. Don't feel bad or guilty, it's the life of a lawman and why would anyone wish for it?"

"Well, that is the thing, now I do. I hate being pressured and seeing others being terrorized, especially women like Kim. She's a good woman and I won't have her treated like that or Nurse Mallory being threatened," he finished firmly.

"Wait, you mean you want the job now? After all that's happened?"

"Yes. That mob down there think that they have the whip hand and everyone must play by their rules. They think they have the place wide open and the mines will be hit next, probably some settlers, too. It's not just sporadic. This is being orchestrated by a clever person or persons unknown. Those are my thoughts, anyway. That being so, I'll be marshal until you're well enough to get back and do the job again. Talking of which, what the hell happened to Lewis last night? He could have at least backed up Clem with a shotgun, bad arm or not," Nate asked indignantly.

"Now that I don't know. It puzzled me and I haven't seen hide nor hair of him since I was bust up. It don't make sense," he stated.

Nate frowned, he wasn't happy with this news, but kept his thoughts to himself.

Gorringe continued: "I will make sure the mayor, judge and senior town council members come up here and we will have an unofficial meeting, then swear you in. Are you still sure? This is a different ball game now, it will be you against the mob."

"I'm certain, after what I have seen at Kim's and Clem... Well enough. I'll do it. One further thing. I want to be a deputy sheriff, too, then I'll have jurisdiction outside the town limits and the right to swear in anyone I like. Agreed?"

"Sure, Nate. No problem at all." Yet the marshal was slightly puzzled. Nate bade him good morning and left. *Something's sure lit a fire under that boy and I know which side I want to be on from now on,* the marshal pondered.

Chapter Twelve

The next day the rumors spread like wildfire: Nate Carlton was back in town and had been appointed marshal and deputy sheriff. Information was sought on his background and the rumors started to spread.

Nate visited the local newspaper, a small concern with a circulation of a few hundred. Yet the copies were sent far and wide. The proprietor was bent over the wooden blocks setting type for this week's edition. Typical of his trade he wore an eye shade, white shirt with black sleeve protectors covering his lower arms. Ink stained fingers stopped working as the bell went and he looked up refocusing over his half-moon spectacles.

"Howdy, what can I do for you?"

"Good morning. I'm the new marshal, Nate Carlton. Wanted to put some business your way if I could?"

"You surely may, what did you have in mind? I'm Geoff Hodges, by the way, proprietor of this rag."

Nate smiled and explained what he wanted. The older

man smiled. "You'll surely light a fire with that, marshal. I hope that you can hang on to what you rope."

"Well, only one way to find out. How long?"

"Come back in an hour and I'll have some ready for you."

Next Nate visited the hardware store and bought a hammer and some tacks. Then got himself a cup of coffee. He could feel an energy building in him, a mix of anger and the surge of a need for action. He hated bullies, and whilst he didn't want the job, the bad element had pushed too far. Another figure came in and Nate watched as he stood inside the door allowing his eyes to adjust to the gloom. He scanned the room and then made for a table near to Nate's. He wore neat range clothes and his hands bore the callouses of rope and gun. A cowhand Nate surmised, and a good one. Yet a Remington Beals sat on his hip, in a well-oiled cut away, tied down holster, set up just right for a fast draw. *Friend or foe?* Nate wondered. He'd heard rumors of more gunmen drifting in and maybe this was one of them.

His doubts were assuaged as the young cowboy sat, ordered a cup of coffee, pushed back his Stetson and smiled over at Nate. "Howdy, friend. Seems like a right lively town you got here from what I heard."

It was an open face with a friendly countenance, tanned by the elements, and the accent was from north of here or Nate missed his guess.

"Well, that's one way of putting it. I might give issue with the friendly, though I hope to resolve that soon. Nate Carlton, newly appointed marshal."

"Howdy, marshal. Morg Newly. Just come down with a

herd to Denver supplying the town and on my way south to see some more country and find some work down there. Thought I'd call in here as I'd heard she was full of life."

"Interesting on the herd. How many head?" Nate asked, keen to talk cattle rather than trouble.

"Oh, only four hundred or so, enough to feed the town and keep everyone stocked. I drifted down from Montana and picked up a riding chore in Cheyenne."

"Ah, thought I caught Montana in there. Well, watch yourself, it's going to get rough before it gets better. Especially with some posters I'm about to put up. I'll see you around, Montana."

"Luck to you, marshal." Morg nodded, raising his coffee cup.

Nate left, first picking up the bag of tacks and the hammer. He picked up the posters from the newspaper office, slipping the thong off the hammer of his Colt, and moved around the town, tacking them up in prominent places. Small clusters of people crowded around each one with gasps and looks in Nate's direction, some shaking their heads. He got back to the hardware store in a circular route seeing a wagon outside apparently stacked with household goods and furniture.

Nate had heard that the Yates's, a small steading family, had been burned out of their home by raiders in the night. The two children were traumatized, and he had planned on riding out there later that day. They were packing a wagon in the main street, loading up supplies for a trip further north and west.

Nate walked up to the wagon seeing the wife sat atop the

bench seat, a sun bonnet on her hair, clothes streaked with soot. "Morning, ma'am, Mister Yates. I'm sorry to hear what happened. I was going to call on you later and see what I could do to help."

The man looked around. His features gaunt, tired and worn out. Dejection built into every line of his body, a man defeated, if ever Nate saw one.

"Too late, mister, we're leaving. Got burned out last night and no law to help," he muttered, anger and resentment in his tone. "Years we spent, puttin' our all into that place, now nothing. Can't hold if'n we don't work it and just two more years to go 'til it's ours from the Homestead Act."

"I can help. I'm the new marshal and deputy sheriff. I can't re-build your home, but I can get the men who did it and make it safe for you."

"You? How're you going to do that? It's bigger than just one man, law or no."

A crowd had gathered around them during this exchange Nate was aware, and before he could answer, a voice came from behind him.

"Yea, how you gonna do that mister marshal, sir? By posting those little bits of paper around so we all doff our hats to you, yes sir, no sir."

Nate turned to face three men in front of the crowd loosely formed in a semi-circle. The speaker was a man who had been at Hart's ranch he was certain, and as if to prove it, Chas Goodman stood at his side. He'd seen him around town, Jennings, that was his name, it came to Nate in a second. He couldn't risk a gunfight with so many people around. There had to be a way round it.

"Well," Nate responded evenly, giving no hint of his thoughts. "I want no trouble. How about I buy you boys a drink and we can discuss this."

The offer of a drink threw them for a few seconds; they had been pushing for trouble and they got humility. "Wa'll, boys, looks like the nice marshal got a streak of yellow, say—"

"Catch!" Nate said, throwing the bag of tacks at one and the hammer at the other. It was instinctive, they couldn't help it: Goodman and Jennings went to catch the objects and the third gunny was transfixed by the action. When they looked back, Nate held both his guns cocked and ready, lined on the three. "Drop the gun belts, boys. Any trouble and I'll shoot you. Frankly it'll save me paperwork and feeding you in jail."

The third man started to wet his lips, he was desperate to make a move. Nate saw it. "You, fancy vest," he said referring to the broad splattered cow hide vest he wore of black, white and tan, "you make one more move towards that gun and I'll kill your friends first and shoot you before you get the gun out. You want to be responsible for killing your friends, go ahead be my guest." There was a hard brittle tone to Nate's words that no one had heard before. "Left hands only, drop them."

"Stew, don't you dare, he means it. But you'll get yours, mister marshal, see if you don't and I'll be there to watch."

They complied, letting their gunbelts drop to the floor.

Not taking his eyes off them Nate asked, "Someone pick up those gun belts. Right, boys move, the jail is just down the street."

He got them inside without incident and slammed the door locking the cells. "You boys just cool off in there."

"When're we getting out?" screamed the one called Stew.

"When I say so, and, when I let you go, don't come back or I'll shoot you on sight."

He turned to see the door open and the cowhand Morg Newly appeared carrying the three gun belts. "Mighty slick work, marshal. Here're the belts."

"Thanks, Montana, much obliged. Don't want a job do you? Pays a hundred a month, better than brush popping," he asked smiling.

"I think I'll give it a miss, but will stick around. I suspect there 'll be more fun yet having read your poster. All those names you've posted to leave, all here in town?"

"Yes they are, and I'm going to do some more house cleaning before tonight gets going or I'll be over run.

"Say, could you just keep an eye on things, whilst I go and see the marshal? I'll be ten minutes, no more."

"I thought you were the marshal?"

"Long story. Ten minutes no more."

"OK, sure."

He had walked to the Gorringe's house and explained all that had occurred and his new notices that had been posted.

"Just one thing. If you go after McCrae, watch him. He won't gunfight you. He'll set you up and that Shillelagh stick he carries. He's fast with it, very fast. Irish stick fightin' they call it, *Bataireacht* or some such. Well, I've seen him whip a man as soon as blink. He's deadly once in range and that range is greater than you might think. So, if he moves in close, watch out!" he warned.

Nate locked this away for the future. "Thank you, noted and I'll be careful."

Nate discussed a few more matters he had in mind including the mine ore. "Seems to me if the ore was shipped, it would take pressure off the mines and with that the town. It wouldn't all be so tangled up and would make it easier to see the wood from the trees."

"Sure, but how you goin' to do it? If you sit up there on that box, as McKenzie wants you, I'll be a prime target and no mistake. Now your idea of outriders might work, but it will still tempt that group of riders out to the north whose tracks you spotted."

"I know, I've been giving it all a lot of thought and have an idea, complicated, but an idea, none the less. I need your views and local knowledge." With which Nate outlined his plan, asking Gorringe questions as he did so.

"It might work," Gorringe said at length, "and you're convinced that there are informers up at the mines giving out information?"

"Definitely, couldn't work otherwise. As I say there's a good brain behind all this, someone who knows their way around the world and its ways, who can see the bigger picture. Well, I'll start by seeing McKenzie, and hear what he has to say. Get well, Marshal, I'll not be here forever," he teased as he closed the door leaving the bedroom.

No, but I've a feeling you might just leave the town in a better state than when you found it— if you survive, young Nate, and I hope that you do. Just one man against the lot of them. Then the marshal shook his head pushing those dark thoughts from his mind.

Nate walked back to the jail to find Morg Newly still there and another visitor: the nester, Yates.

"Thanks, Morg, I appreciate you minding the store for me."

"My pleasure, it's all been quiet apart from those yahoos mouthing off. I told them to be quiet or they'd get no food, seemed to cool them off a might. This here gent came into see you." He nodded at Yates who stood there, his hat in his hand.

"I guess you are the marshal, kinda doubted it for a while back there, never saw the like. You sure handed that lot their needings. You're mighty fast." He looked down at the gun on Nate's hip. "Did you mean what you said about protecting me and my family? 'Cause I figure if anyone can, you can do it."

"I did, Mister Yates. Listen, why don't I ride out with you now, if you are going back. Make sure everything is settled and no one is there to bother you."

"I'd appreciate that, marshal. My name is Graham and I thank you."

"Good. Are there any neighbors who can help you nearby, Graham? Get a shelter up, things like that?"

"Sure, the Palmers and Foxes. They tried to dissuade me from leaving, if I told 'em I was back, I'm sure they'd help get me fixed in the short term."

"Good, well let's get started then. I'll get my horse and we'll head out straight away." He then turned to Morg Newly, smiling. "Oh, Morg, would you like to—"

"I know, I know," he said mournfully, "look after the store and you'll be right back. Well as long as I get to sit here loafing and get paid for it. Fair enough. Do I get a badge and such?"

"Raise your right hand. Do you swear... oh hell, just say 'I do'."

"I do."

"Excellent, you are now an official deputy marshal of Langtonville. Oh, and if a man comes in with his arm in a sling claiming to be a deputy name of Tye Lewis, don't take any stick from him and tell him he's fired, pending my return."

Morg raised his hands shrugging. "Anything you say, marshal. I'll just be asleep on the bunk here." He winked.

Nate laughed as he left, followed by Yates and went to fetch his horse.

Chapter Thirteen

Nate had no idea where the Yates's farm was so just followed the wagon with the two plow horses tied to the back. He wanted no conversation, just time to consider all that had gone on and what his next move would be. He was surprised to see them head towards the mines, then skirt wide to the north to be about ten miles north east of where he had ridden the day before on his return from the mesa. They could not take the shortcut through the cutting of the knoll as it was unsuitable for a wagon, only for horses or mules, and therefore the journey took much longer.

The ground he saw was red clay and soil, caught between two walls of sandstone giving protection from the north and a small stream trickled its way through the pasture land. As they neared what was left of the house he saw that Yates had dammed it and dug a wide area to form a shallow pond for watering stock and irrigating his land.

It was a good spot and the charred remains of the farm-house stood on a slightly raised position, sitting on red rock in the lee of a clutch of aspens that blew in the breeze and would offer shade to the corral and stock. Two milk cows lay dead and bloated in the sun and a howl went up as a dark haired mongrel appeared, limping as it came forward managing a low rising bark. Spirals of smoke drifted skywards from the blackened ruins, yet still one end of the house stood, supported by the stone chimney that had withstood the blaze and supported the end wall and two sides of the original house. It would offer temporary shelter and a lean-to, Nate surmised.

One of the children on the wagon shrieked and made to jump down, shouting, "Blackie!"

"Wait, boy, let me go first. I need to be sure all is well," Nate urged.

Nate had shucked his Spencer from the scabbard and held it cocked and ready across the saddle swell. He looked around, nothing stirred and the mongrel seemed unaware of anybody else there. Yet he was still unsure. He scanned the hill into the distance and between a knoll and saw the outline of two riders that had suddenly come into view, driving a small herd of cows before them. Upon seeing the party at the house, they left the cows and spurred on down the hill.

Nate didn't hesitate, he dropped down off Buck and squatted down behind the water trough making a smaller target, taking a bead with his Spencer. When they got within forty feet, he shouted: "That's enough, boys. Hold it right there and raise your hands."

They skidded their horses to a halt, no liking the argument of a drawn Spencer, as Nate rose from behind the trough.

"What's the matter, mister, no call for a rifle on us. We're just driving some cows onto the land that belongs to our boss."

Nate circled slightly seeing the brands of the horses. "Circle Hart, eh? Listen, boys, I'm giving you the benefit of the doubt. I'm Nate Carlton, the new marshal and deputy sheriff of Langtonville. These people behind me own and farm here, they, as you can see were burnt out last night. You boys do that?" he asked, a hard edge to his voice.

"No!" exclaimed one, "we just had orders to ride over with them cows as the land was now free, we were told. Had nothin' to do with burnin' anyone out, we're just cowhands, not gun hands, take orders and herd cattle."

"Then you must know who did," Nate responded unrelenting. "Who was missing last night on the Circle?"

"Oh, a few of the boys went to town—" the one began.

"Shut up, Curly. We didn't see no one missing, Marshal," the lanky cowhand said after cutting the other off abruptly.

Nate shook his head. "Right, if that's the way you want it. Get off your horses, now."

The two men looked at each other and dismounted, at which Nate told them to drop their guns and take the rifles from their scabbards. They complained bitterly cursing him.

Nate stepped forward, emptied the six guns bar two loads each, picked up the rifles and stepped back. He threw the two pistols to the cowhands who caught them shoving them into their belts. "Now you go back to your boss, with your cows. You've got two rounds each, for rattlers and to dissuade any Indians. But not enough to get you into any trouble. I don't want you laying for me or Yates, here, and tell your boss, or Brannon, he is to be left alone. Understand?"

"Brannon didn't send us, it was—" Again he was silenced.

"What about our rifles?" asked the lanky cowhand.

"You come into town tomorrow, you can have them back."

They muttered and cursed him under their breath, agreed with a surly nod, remounted and headed back to the small herd.

"Thank you, marshal. I do appreciate it," Yates said.

"Now Billy, you can go to your dog," Nate said with a smile.

The family disembarked the wagon, Mrs. Yates in tears at seeing her house in ruins again. Then she wiped them away stoically and turned to Nate thanking him.

"My pleasure, it was the least I could do, ma'am, and please call me Nate." He then sent Graham Yates off to fetch his neighbors and set about helping clear the immediate wreckage and see what could be salvaged of the structure.

Two hours later Yates returned with his neighbors, one with a wagon containing some lumber and tools, at which they set to with a will and an urgency. Nate made to leave urging them to be on the lookout and keep their guns ready, then a thought occurred. "I forgot to ask. The boundary of your land, does it stretch to the foothills yonder that form the other half of the mining hills?"

"Why sure," Yates answered, "my land goes all the way to the foothills. But I rarely go the way on account of the canyon, it sort of splits the land. I keep meaning to bridge it, but it will take time and money. You have to go out of your way to the south, then there is a natural steep trail down and back up, not easy but a good horse can do it. Reckon I've only been there a few times since we owned the place. Why'd you ask?"

"Oh, just curious. I might go back that way."

"Well, head south, for about two miles, then you'll see a dip and sorta red arroyo. Follow that downhill and then it makes a break to the left on a switchback, from then on the trail is clear, but steep, so watch yourself," Yates urged.

Nate bade them goodbye with a kiss on the cheek from Dot Yates and a smile of deep gratitude in her eyes.

However, it works out, he pondered as he rode away, *it's good to be helping people if nothing else.*

Nate followed the directions coming to the arroyo and dropped down scouting the land. This trail had hardly been used for anything other than by game and the occasional coyote, yet there was a set of horse tracks, newly imprinted, shod at that, no Indian made them, he noticed. The track was all Yates said it would be and within half an hour of steady descending and climbing he found himself almost where he had been yesterday on the other side; it was wild country and the canyon had been dark and cool in the heat of the day. A small stream lay at the bottom that had, over hundreds of years eroded away at the land to create that deep chasm. Nate was willing to bet that flash floods still screamed through the canyon and would kill anything in its path with the water level running high and fast. None would want to be caught in that valley bottom in such conditions.

He rode on and there before him was the fork which led

to the new workings he had discovered yesterday. So near and yet so far and obscured. Clever. Whoever was behind these works knew what they were doing. Nate pushed on wanting to make sure that he returned to town as soon as possible, yet he had one more job to accomplish that day: a meeting with Mackenzie.

He crested the knoll and this time dropped down into the mining camp. The camp was live with shouts, jack hammers and the odd explosion from blasting into the hills or from below as the ground vibrated beneath. Buck sidled and half passed, not liking the tremors beneath his hooves, his first instinct being to run from the perceived 'earth-quake'. Nate steadied him with a gentle hand and clamped his legs upon his flanks through the fenders of his saddle, reassuring the stallion. Nate wended his way through the small town of tents, shacks, cooking fires, chutes and troughs to the center of the camp, where stood the stone blockhouse that he helped defend in the night raid.

A guard with a rifle was stationed outside and upon Nate's arrival called a greeting and shouted for whoever was inside to come out. As Nate stepped down from the saddle, McKenzie's long frame stooped to emerge from the restricted doorway that was deliberately low to impede easy access and make it more difficult to raid.

"Well good day to ye, laddie. Or should that be Marshal Carlton now?" he chided.

"Well, Nate will do. Just fine thank you. Have you got a minute to chat? I have some ideas on what we discussed about shipping the ore."

McKenzie's face was a play of emotions as he looked

around to see who was listening, confused and worried. "Come in then, come in and I'll get you a cup of coffee, or would you prefer tea as it's the afternoon?"

Nate agreed and tethered his horse to the hitching rail outside the blockhouse, ducking his head as he entered, heeding the warning of two steps down to the lowered floor inside. Once within, he found he was easily able to stand upright and it was cool against the heat of the day. It was well set up with one wall given over to a steel cell similar to a jail, within were piles of sacks containing ore ready for shipping. No windows were on that side, and those that were evident, had thick steel bars at the windows. Rough wooden steps gave access to a flat roof via a trap door, that was lined with steel plate.

It was a fortress, he decided, and a further guard was in evidence within, sitting by the locked door of the cage. Another was on the roof, behind the parapet wall that surmounted the entire blockhouse.

"Please have a seat," McKenzie offered as he made tea using a small stove that lay near a window, allowing the heat to escape. "Now before we go any further, I need to get some others of the syndicate in here."

"I have a better idea," Nate interjected, "why don't you make the tea and then you and I will go for a wander around the mines and you can show me what's what."

McKenzie gave him a searching look as he realized what Nate wanted.

With tea made and carrying two tin mugs, they made their way outside to wander around the camp. As they got to the foothills and away from earshot, Nate began to explain in more detail what he was proposing.

"You feel this can be done?" McKenzie asked, impressed with what he proposed.

"I do, and another thing. Have you or any of the teams here begun mining on the other side of the hills, to the right of the knoll yonder?" He nodded with his head in the direction he meant.

"Where, over there?" McKenzie went to point but Nate cut him off. "No, don't point. Yes, that knoll between the two humps of the hill. There is a narrow trail through there."

"Och, I may have ridden there once or twice but never to prospect and no one has registered a claim there. We thought it didna look right and this was providing rich seams here, so why give ourselves a headache and it'd be a nightmare to transport ore back around much further and more isolated. So no, why do you ask?"

Nate explained what he'd seen and found out about the ownership. McKenzie was surprised and dismayed. "You think someone is mining there on Yates's land?"

"I do and this could be part of the key to the whole business."

McKenzie tugged gently at his trimmed beard, lost in thought. "Very well, let me think on it and I'll come into town to discuss how and when it might be organised."

"Just one more thing, Tam," Nate continued suddenly very serious. "Don't tell anyone about the mining over the hill or my other proposals. Just about the stagecoach run and my plans for that. Your life and fortune will depend upon it, of that I'm certain. No matter how much you feel you can trust anyone, not a word, are we agreed?"

McKenzie gave him a hard stare and made a decision. "Alright, my word on it. But I dinna believe anyone here would betray us." He spat on his hand and offered the calloused palm to be shook by Nate.

Nate shook it, arched an eyebrow and offered: "Yea, and that's what the citizens of Troy believed, too."

With that he turned and just then Si Holder marched up. "Now have you changed your mind, for I see that you are a marshal now. My offer still stands," he said smiling at Nate, who explained why he had come with an abbreviated version.

"Well, we might just be in business, but I'll let McKenzie give you all the details. I must be off back to town. See you soon, McKenzie." With that he wheeled Buck and pushed into a slow lope keen to get back to town and see what damage had been done.

Chapter Fourteen

Riding close to Langtonville, Nate circled round the back from the north, not keen to advertise his presence; dropped Buck back at the livery barn giving him a rub down and some hard feed as he had earned it. Then he entered the marshal's office by the back door from the rear alley, asking to be let in by Morg who had locked the rear door.

"Thought you'd done lit out on me and headed for Texas," he joshed.

"I'm sorry, Morg, it took me longer than I thought. The Yates's place certainly is a mess." He then explained what he had found and who he had met, including the run in with the Circle riders.

"You got more trouble coming. There've been cat calls and shouts at the jail that McCrae has been tearing down your posters and reckons to settle with you personally. Claims that if you want him shut down, you'd better do it yourself and that he's waiting for you."

"Well, he can stew for a while, he'll keep. Listen, do you

need anything? Go get a meal on me. Then come back if you would and look after things just while I change and wash up." He pushed a five dollar bill into Morg's hand and told him to treat himself.

"Nate, you got yourself a deal."

Nate then slumped into a chair, thought better of it and made for the couch to the side of the office, away from the separate door to the cells. Whoever had built this setup knew what they were doing he surmised. Feeling exhausted he realized that he would need to be on good form this evening. After an hour, he heard knocking at the door and let Morg back in.

"A powerful lot of feeling building out there. If you was being nominated for mayor I don't think you'd win many votes. Even the odd townsman is nervous."

"Can't be helped. I'll run it my way or no way." He was feeling much more refreshed and ready. "I'll be back in an hour. I promise," he said seeing Morg's look of disbelief.

"Well that was good a meal at the Northern Star so I won't argue none."

Nate left by the back door and returned to the livery stable. A few days ago he had set up a used burlap sack which he stuffed with old saddle blankets and straw. He had used it daily as a punch bag away from prying eyes, putting into practice all the moves of kicks and punches that his father and Michel Casseux had taught him. Like gunfighting, practice and stretching were an important part of any fighting method. After half an hour later he was warm, stretched and in the mode that fighters seek, ready mentally, as well as physically.

Satisfied he left, moving along the back lanes and alleys to arrive at Kim's. Letting himself in, he saw her and ordered a meal. She was pleased to see him and provided steak, beans and mashed potatoes. He wolfed it down not knowing how hungry he had been. He went to his room and changed, put in half an hour's practice with his colts and came back to the jail unnoticed.

Somehow word must have got out as the sun was starting to dip, bringing a warm breeze on the evening air. "Montana, would you go and get word to the mayor for me and the judge?" He scribbled a quick note and passed it across, giving him directions to the mayor's house.

A deputation of two councilors, Mayor Roberts and Judge Raybold arrived shortly thereafter.

"Thank you for coming, gentlemen. Let me be frank. Today I'm going to be tested. McCrae has been boasting and can't back down. They want to break me. I know it's coming. They'll lure me down there to the Barrel on some pretext, probably a shooting and set me up. Now, all I'm asking is that you keep me from getting back shot. Don't come with me, don't get in my way. Just leave me to handle it. I need you there before I get shot, not like poor Clem."

The four men looked sheepishly at him, knowing that they had erred in judgement. They all agreed to his request. "Now I don't want a gunfight. I want a show of solidarity for me and law and order. If you don't want it and can't handle it, let me know and I'll walk."

"We'll back you, Nate, you have our word," Judge Raybold said as the others nodded in agreement.

They all had long guns which he knew were a very

persuasive argument at short range and the curmudgeonly old judge had a shotgun, in the crook of his arm. "Good, now go back to your homes and as soon as you hear shooting come to the source and we'll see how we go, but keep back and let me handle it."

An hour later gunfire sounded through the air emanating from the Barrel saloon. Nate permitted himself a tight smile. "Montana, I don't want you getting killed or hurt on my behalf. You've helped me enough giving me a break to do what I needed to do and put some things right for Yates. Don't get involved anymore. Just stay here—"

"And mind the store. I know, yea like hell I will. I never yet got into something I didn't want to and I can handle my end in a gunfight. So we'll just leave her as she is, and see how the cards fall," he assured Nate.

Nate thanked him and went to the gun rack, taking down a Colt revolving shotgun which he tossed to the young cowhand. "I've checked and oiled it. It works fine and is loaded for bear. Man I knew, once said it was the best way to control a crowd." *And I sure wish he was here tonight,* Nate thought to himself. Saying out loud, he added, "...and he was a ranger, so he'd know.

"Right, let's see what that nice Mr. McCrae has planned for us." Nate picked up a new Winchester '66 off the rack, that would be quicker to lever shells and better for use in the town than his old Spencer, where its bullets would easily travel through thick wooden walls and kill someone on the other side. The rifle that was fast becoming known as a Yellow Boy, because of its distinctive brass frame, shone dully in the fading light.

They left the jail locking the door and moved off carefully down the street with a quick wave at the approaching party of townsmen, who were there to back him up.

Nate felt a tension ease from his body. He had been holding himself tightly, now with action it started to release. It was good to be moving again. He watched Morg walk down the opposite side of the sidewalk slightly behind him, constantly looking, left, right and upwards.

It was still light enough to see well, although the ongoing dusk was casting long shadows across the street, with a few oil lamps having been lit. There was a great deal of noise coming from the far end hailing from the Barrel saloon. Nate could feel the strain building in him, trying to plan in his mind how he would see this through.

Closing in on the saloon he saw a man, clearly on watch, dart inside as he approached. He signaled for Morg to stay outside and cover his back. He stepped inside the huge canvas tent going left as soon as he entered, staying as much in the shadow as he could, as his eyes adjusted. The noise slowly petered out, as everyone turned to see him standing there. A bouncer stood to his left by a table and another gunman or house man certainly to his eyes, stood to his right. Others were dotted about the floor, each eyeing him and waiting for instructions from their boss McCrae, who stood at the bar, balancing on his stick, yet of course seeming to stand easily.

"Well, good evening marshal, nice of you to join us. Will you have a drink? To sort of celebrate your promotion."

The crowd laughed at the weak joke, eyes expectant. It

was a tough crowd and any of them would plug him if they thought they could get away with it.

There would be a distraction Nate knew, then a closing, all seemingly in fun or good nature, but by then it would be too late. He would be smothered or muffled, closed down, unable to use his guns and then he would die.

"No. You're coming with me, McCrae," he snapped. *Here it comes*, he thought.

The nearby gunman rose from his seat, hand extended in a gesture of friendship. "Oh, come on, marshal, that's not very friendly. We just wanna buy you a drink and all. Look—" He began extending his arm as he moved forward.

Nate sensed rather than saw the bouncer to his left begin to move, his Winchester in both hands, barrel pointing upwards, held casually. It was this that the gunman was going for. Nate had to move now and he did. He swung the stock across smashing into the face of the gunman, breaking his jaw with a crack; then continuing the turn, lowered the rifle, sliding the barrel straight into the oncoming bouncer, crushing his throat. He collapsed like a landed fish gasping for air. Nate moved again, to stand beside one of the thick uprights supporting the tent, levered a shell into the breach and pointed it straight at McCrae.

"Now, McCrae, you've had your fun with your gunnies, get over here and I promise all of you; you might get me, but I take a lot of killing and the first to be downed will be your boss.

"Now you've been posted to leave town and boasted you wouldn't. That's enough to arrest you. So get over here and come with me to the jail."

A glint of defiance entered McCrae's eyes: "You goin' to shoot me in cold blood? You're a marshal not a murderer. Come and get me." He grinned wickedly, knowing that the twenty feet to the bar would give every opportunity to have someone in the crowd kill or maim him.

Nate said nothing, he had foreseen this and reached up to one of the oil lamps hanging on the nail above his head, his right hand still steady on the breach of the Winchester.

"Now you come or I burn you and this crowd of killers, card sharps and scum out. Your choice."

McCrae's face held a look of disbelief. "You wouldn't dare!" He knew it would go up like a tinder box and everyone looked around nervously ready to run from the huge tent with its rough wooden planked floors.

"Try me, on three: one, two..."

"Alright, I'll come, I'll come, but you'll regret this, marshal." With which he limped over towards the entrance leaning on his stick, fury written across his pugnacious features. His broad shoulders rolled easily as he walked, with surprising grace for a man with a bad leg, Nate observed.

"Coming out, Morg, make way. McCrae following me."

"Got it covered, Nate, and the others are here, too. All ringed around. And tell him the gunny he had waiting at the side is having second thoughts. Well he will do when he wakes up."

McCrae scowled at this. He had assumed that Nate would be alone and would find an opportune moment to leap in or take him unawares. Getting within a few feet he halted and said: "You're a big man with that gun in your hand hiding behind your badge, Carlton. You wouldn't dare

139

face me without it. Why, I bet you wouldn't." With this he took a step and the blackwood stick came up as if to point.

Gorringe's warning screamed at Nate. He was only just in time. The nobbled end flew out where his head had been as McCrae took a quick agile step forward, on balance and lethal.

Nate reacted the only way he knew how, firing from the hip with his Navy, having let go of the rifle with his right hand. He drew and fired by instinctive alignment at a range that was difficult to miss as the stick was drawn back again, level and parallel to the large Irishman's chest, ready to flick out again with the speed of a rattler's head. The bullet caught the stick, midway, directing it upwards with the trajectory, jerking his right hand back with a snap. He howled in pain as the wrist twisted with the force of the impact.

"You're a fraud and a coward, McCrae. You pretend to be tough, but hide behind a stick and your tough thugs. You and all that Frisco' Barbary Coast dry gulchers. Without your saps, sticks and knock out drugs, you're nothing," Nate taunted. He knew what was coming and wanted him angry and scorned in front of his crowd, for that would make him careless.

"Why, you jumped up kid. I'll rip your head off and take out your eyes, if you gave me half a chance, without your guns!" he roared.

"You follow me out then. you coward. We'll settle this on the street away from your gunnies and billy canes, if you think you can." Nate sneered at him.

McCrae nearly threw himself bodily at Nate despite the

Navy Colt lined on him. "I'm coming, marshal sir," he said, his accent getting thicker with anger. "And I'm gonna to rip your Rebel head off."

Nate went outside the tent, moving warily, standing aside to see a loose semi-circle of men stood around the entrance. Morg was there, so were the townsmen all armed and keeping control.

Nate flipped the Colt back into its holster all the while watching McCrae, undid the pigging thong from his leg, unbuckled the gun belt and handed it and his Stetson to Judge Raybold.

"Come on then, you Irish bog trotter, come and get me." And Nate threw a punch straight to his head, only it didn't land. McCrae knew what he was doing, stepped in and swatted it aside with ease, throwing a straight right from his hip that seemed to come from nowhere, catching Nate in the wind. He doubled over with pain bringing his elbows up as he did in a reflex action, just as McCrae's knee came driving up to pulp his face. If it had landed with full force, the fight would have ended then and there. Nate rolled backwards, desperate for air into his lungs. He had underestimated the man, thinking he was just a brawler, yet his experience in the bar fights and riverboats of the Coast had stood him well. The scar tissue around his eyes and the rough ears all told stories.

McCrae followed him, laughing as he did. "Now, you Rebel scum. I'm going beat you to death, but first I'm gonna to break your gunfighter's hands."

Nate went to push up from the floor just as a hard boot heel drove down to crush his hand. He did the unexpected and dived forward catching the leg and pulling as he went, twisting the foot the wrong way. McCrae went crashing down to land on his side, and Nate used the time well to get to his feet and drag air into his lungs. He had been hit before when he had boxed with his father and sparred at Savate with Michel Casseux, knowing what he had to do.

McCrae jumped to his feet, weaving now with his fists, keen to get at the smaller man. He suddenly plunged in with a feint of his left, again throwing the deadly right from the hip, this time driving up for the chin as the guard was open. Nate crossed with his left elbow, taking the blow on the forearm, yet such was the power behind it that it drove it back to his chest. *Damn, the man can punch,* he thought off handedly. This was different from any normal bar fight or the rough and tumble of school fights. This was a deadly battle to the end with no quarter given.

Two more crosses followed. One made him see stars and step back, hitting the hitching rail in his lower back, just as McCrae came forward to stomp him with a forward stamp to his stomach.

Using the rail, Nate vaulted out of the way as the foot missed, landing McCrae against the rail, both hands stopping him to keep his balance. Nate joined his hands, swinging round in an axe blow straight to McCrae's kidneys. It was a wicked blow, his back arching in pain. Nate went for a follow up, but the huge man was game, turning to block with his elbow and came back swinging, left and right, each blow driving Nate back with the force of each blocked punch. The third hit home, bouncing off his turned shoulder, smashing into his ear. It hurt and rang bells in his head. Then he danced off left, needing the distance.

A terrible rage was building in him. His English father had always taught him never to lose his temper, fight yes, but with control. Now his inner demons were being unleashed, with a loss of all reason. He had felt it during the war and seen others go berserk in battle, not knowing what they did, just with a lust to kill; a terrible hatred in their hearts in battle madness. Nate was losing now he knew, and to lose was to die or worse be broken, a cripple, with no hands and blinded.

Twice more the Irishman stepped in swinging then driving with that evil shot off his hip, hurting him each time. Then he feinted, and grasped Nate in a bear hug at his lower back, bending and crushing him with all his brutal force.

McCrae's head was tucked down with no room for a Liverpool kiss as Nate writhed in his awful embrace seeking release from the pain. He then twisted his head in a final effort, sought and found a cauliflower ear, clamping his teeth upon it biting hard. The man howled as the teeth severed it, ripping at the flesh. There it was, the raised nose. Nate smashed the bridge of his forehead down once, twice, hearing the cartilage crack and blood flow, and with that the pressure released. He drove his knee up, smashing not quite between McCrae's legs as he turned to avoid the knee, but with enough damage to cause him to give loss of grip and Nate wrenched free.

Desperate for space, the wounded bloody animal before him roared in pain, breathing hard through his open mouth, blood running from ear and nose. "Oh, now I'm gonna kill you, boy."

Nate danced backwards getting his back working again, once, twice he danced away as the big hammer blows came in, landing but not with full force. Then he planted his feet, hands apart, left forward as if to invite a straight to his unguarded front. His feet were wide apart, the right, drawn back.

McCrae roared in sensing victory, stepping with the left again to launch that awesome hip punch.

Nate twisted his upper torso, spinning on the ball of his left foot, driving the right round in a low roundhouse to catch the back of McCrae's leg right over the sciatic nerve with the sharp point of his cowboy boot.

Agony shot through McCrae as the leg collapsed in pain. Yet Nate did not stop, he wanted to destroy and there was no mercy in him. Again he drove it up whipping once, twice more, faster than the eye could follow, each time for the tender vulnerable nerve. "Now you'll need your stick!" he shouted, all reason lost as the Irishman collapsed onto one knee barely conscious.

Then Nate smashed his elbow down into the point where the jaw hinges, unhinging the joint and sending him into oblivion. McCrae dropped unconscious at Nate's feet, but he didn't stop. So enraged was he and fueled with adrenalin, Nate bent forward to pick up his head by the hair, wanting to smash and destroy, lost in the red mist of battle. Gentle but firm hands gripped him: "Stop, Nate, stop, you've won!" Morg urged. "Nate, back off, you'll kill him!"

Finally, he calmed down looking unfocused at Morg

with incomprehension, then his shoulders sagged, as he gazed at the supine unconscious figure lying on the floor. The crowd was in awe. No one had believed that he would last, let alone win the fight against the huge Irishman.

"OK, I'm fine, thank you." He shook his head which was still ringing from the battering he took. Then he looked around, his eyes still murderous. He turned reaching for a bucket of water that always stood by the entrance to the huge saloon tent. He picked it up and before anyone could stop him he threw it over McCrae, who spluttered and came to, eyes struggling to focus, pain suddenly apparent to his befuddled brain, hand instinctively going to his sagging jaw.

"McCrae, I told you to leave town and take your scum with you. Now you will see the consequences."

Again, he reached for the oil lamp off one of the wooden poles supporting the entrance canopy. Without hesitation he smashed it on the floor at the bottom of the tent skirts. The oil spread and immediately ignited, flames licking hungrily at the bone-dry material, which was instantly consumed by the blaze. "Best get out now, boys, she's alight!" he shouted inside the tent.

Most customers had come outside to see the fight, but a few bouncers and gunmen had hung back to see from within and mind the bar. Now there were shouts of alarm and fear as the blaze took hold, rising high into the early evening.

McCrae gave an animalistic howl of "Nooooo!" distorted by his broken face and tried to rise and save his kingdom.

Mayor Roberts shouted at Nate: "You're mad, the town will go up."

"No it won't. There's no wind and it's far enough away from the main buildings, just watch out for stray sparks." He gestured at the nearby wooden structures that were thirty feet away, as the saloon tent was set back and away on the outskirts of town. Men ran to get water from the troughs and return with a small fire pump pulled by horses ready to douse any flames that sprang up.

Nate took his gun belt and buckled it with unsteady hands, collecting the Winchester from Morg: "You all watched a man die in front of this scum. A good man. You came too late to help him, if at all. These are the consequences. All those posted on that bill, get out by tomorrow morning or you're in jail. I want a clean town and by God, I'll get it. I'll be at the jail if anyone wants me. Doc, sort this dog out, either here or at the jail and once you're done, if he can be moved, he'll be on a horse and out of here," Nate shouted.

Nate strode off into the evening gloom casting a long shadow thrown by the light of the blaze. Morg was at his back covering him until Nate reached the sidewalk where he turned and did the same for Morg.

Once again in the cover of the buildings he relaxed slightly as the pair made their way to the jailhouse.

Chapter Fifteen

The pair arrived at the jail unscathed, glad to be back in the shadows where they could relax with a solid wall at their backs.

Morg shook his head. "Waal, I would never have believed it if'n I hadn't seen with my own eyes. Mister, you've got some gumption and grit, I'll give you that. Mind, you've made a bad enemy that is still alive. Maybe I should have let you kill him, anyways. 'Cause it'll come to that one day, sure as hell. That sort is a hater who bears a grudge and it warn't no normal brawl. I swear I've never seen anything so brutal. You both wanted to kill each other."

Nate tilted his head nodding. "That we did. I lost my temper, terrible thing. I don't believe I've made many friends even with the townsmen. They'll not like me for burning that tent. But it had to be done for many reasons, but I want to thank you Morg for backing me up and pulling me off, I really appreciate it.

"Now," he continued, "the night is young and they'll

be stunned for a while but more trouble will be brewing, now I've set a hare running. I, or rather we need to be seen." He cut off briefly running to a nearby bucket puking into it. He came up looking pale and green at the same time. "Damn, he could punch, every blow hurt even those that I blocked. I'll be a stiff as hell tomorrow. Now, I've got to see to my hands." He looked down at them constantly flexing his fingers, not daring to stop less they seize up.

A pump was set by a sink at the back and here he went to run cold water on them. The cool water was soothing. He then worked them back and forth, took out some tight black leather gloves from a drawer of the desk that he used to spar in. He was about to try to pull them on as he dried his hands, when a knock sounded at the rear dear.

"It's me, Cal from the livery."

Morg opened the door and returned with the wiry old timer from the livery barn, who held a bottle of thick, murky liquid in his hands. "Heard about the fight, thought you might need some of this." He raised the bottle. "Horse liniment, but durned good on humans too, well those that are sufferin'. Mind, she don't go easy on you, it'll burn a might, but get the stiffness out sure enough," he mumbled, through a half toothless smile.

"Thank you, Cal, I'll try it. My hands are certainly stiffening. I'm obliged to you."

"No problem. I'll be back out, don't want to be seen here. Elements around town won't take kindly to it." He winked and shuffled off with his bow legged gait, back to the door and was gone.

Nate unstopped the bottle and took a careful sniff and winced, pulling back quickly. "Well, it'll either kill or cure!"

Morg poured a small amount of the thick concoction onto Nate's hands and he rubbed it well. Within seconds it started to heat up, with a strong smell permeating the room. Within a minute his hands were tingling with heat, but movement was returning, as he continued to flex them.

"Well, it's working and I'm still alive," he joshed. Nate put the gloves on and hefted the Winchester. "I can still use this, it'll be enough. You still with me as my unofficial deputy?"

"I'm still here, ain't I?" he said.

"That you are."

Then the door was pushed open and in stepped Tye Lewis the absent deputy who had not been seen since Clem's death.

"You! Where have you been? We could have used you this evening," Nate said accusingly.

The look of surprise on the deputy's face was a picture. He had not been expecting Nate, especially upright and evidently in good health. "Well, I've been recovering, see. 'Cause of my arm." He whined plaintively rotating his shoulder.

"Tough. You're out. Go back to whoever is paying you. Because it isn't this town. You let Clem down now he's dead and you killed him as assuredly as if you pulled the trigger."

The pitiful expression changed to a sneer: "You. You'll get yours, see if you don't. Think you're the big man having beaten McCrae? Well, there's more trouble coming, gun trouble and you're in deep."

"Two of us, and I shoot just as well as any gunman," Morg said calmly, eyes unflinchingly meeting those of Lewis's.

"Yea? Well, we'll see." With that he turned and stormed back out.

"That you, Lewis?" came a call from the open door to the rear cells.

"No, your tame deputy has run away. Sorry, boys, I'm still here for now," Nate mocked them. "You take that shotgun and we'll do the rounds and shock them..." He ran for the bucket once more to throw up, swilled some water around his mouth and spat it into the sink.

"You sure about this?" Morg asked.

"I am. They'll be thinking I'm licking my wounds and beaten up. They won't be expecting me to be up and about. Even for a short while it will keep them thinking and off balance." But privately Nate admitted that he felt awful and every muscle ached. And who he considered, were 'they'? He was still no nearer to getting to the power behind all this, as he was convinced someone was pulling the strings. Was it Isobel's father? He pondered this, hoping against hope that it wasn't.

They left the jail locking the door behind them and taking the key to the cells. They started going down one side of the street checking doors were locked and windows secure, moving from shadow to shadow. Their eyes and ears were open for any trouble. They called in at the Pair of Aces saloon, pushing open the batwing doors to stand either side as they went in looking over the crowd, who suddenly became silent with a few gasps of surprise as they spotted Nate.

"Marshal," called the owner, a well upholstered man with a tight vest buttoned around his portly frame and piggy eyes that missed nothing. "May I congratulate you on your victory over McCrae. It was some fight, I hear. Let me buy you a celebratory drink."

"Well, he was breaking the law, as I'm sure you are aware," Nate commented drily ignoring the offer. "I see that certain men I put on that list are sat over there at that table. I need them out of here now and on a horse and out of town." He looked pointedly at a table of four tough looking men, who dropped their cards, swiveling their chairs to look over at Nate.

"Come and arrest us then, marshal, because we ain't goin'," one of them said pushing back his chair giving access to the pistol at his hip.

Nate brought the rifle straight up to his shoulder, aiming directly at the man who had spoken, as all those in the way scattered, hunting cover: "Mister, this is a Winchester '66, shoots very straight and frankly I can't miss at this range. I won't kill you but I'll mess up your shoulder really well. Now drop your gun belts or you'll never use them again."

The men complied scowling as they did so. "Now one at a time over here. You, loud mouth, go first."

They all came forward, until under Morg's watchful eye they moved out onto the street. Nate then shoved them forward at gunpoint back to the jail. Then they found a problem.

"Nate, there's only one cell half empty. What're we gonna do?"

Nate smiled and told him. He had been considering this over the last few minutes. He told Morg what he wanted him to do, as the prisoners were now lying face down on the floor. Minutes later with much noise and cussing they were in the corridor shackled to the bars of the jail cells. They started getting raucous and noisy complaining of their treatment.

"If you boys want to keep that up all night, I'll shackle you outside to the bars of the windows, throw a bucket of water over you and let you stand all night shivering! You think that I won't carry out my threat, just keep singing and annoying me and you will see," he finished, grinning wickedly.

They looked at each other wondering whether to call his bluff. And decided against it, quietening down.

With the prisoners locked up, Nate decided that he was going to finish the rounds by himself. Word would have got around that he was fine and had dealt with some of the rabble on the list, so the rest of the evening should be uneventful, he hoped. Still, he left by the back door, skirting alleys and keeping off the main street, where he would be an obvious target. He found himself by the back entrance to the Northern Star saloon. There was a small backyard here as it was one of the older properties; a lean-to and a corral off it.

Nate was about to move on, when the door opened throwing a pool of light onto the yard and a trace of perfume floated on the air as a shadowy figure was silhouetted and a tiny spark of light from a cigarette could just be seen. The perfume was good quality and familiar, it would be Candy, he surmised.

He was about to move out of the shadows and say good evening when hoofbeats were heard and a rider appeared, stiff backed in the manner of an easterner or cavalry officer. The horse was guided to the corral, where the rider dismounted: "Good evening, Candy, you were expecting me, I see." The voice was friendly, well mannered and belonged, Nate recognized, to Charles Hart, Isobel's father and owner of the Circle Hart ranch.

"I was, it's Friday, isn't it? I'm sure that Moises will be along in a minute. Jackson's already inside. He's drinking so he's becoming careless. We need to get him into my private room soon."

Nate was surprised and pleased that he had heard this. He knew Hart came to town to the Star and everyone assumed it was for some female company. This seemed much more. Moises? Why did the name ring a bell? Then he recalled Hart's banker with the nephew coming to stay. Isobel had told him. *Late for a meeting with your banker,* Nate ruminated. *And who was Jackson?*

He moved off deciding that he might be better served by entering from the front, as part of his nightly rounds. He went up onto the side walk and peered in through one of the windows, not wishing to be noticed.

He was in time to see Candy motion to a man who was sat at a table near the back, playing cards and nursing a bottle of whiskey. A saloon girl was draped across his shoulders, attentive and adoring in her manner. Nate saw a man of around thirty, with tanned features, cut in series of angles, with black hair and a thick drooping moustache, covering all his upper lip and down below the corners of his mouth. He wore range clothes yet was clearly no cowhand. He looked vicious and tough, with hard dark eyes that had no mercy in them. The man who Nate assumed was Jackson, rose, throwing down his hand having lost, scowled at the rest of the players and gave a kiss to the girl who pocketed a folded bill and smiled up at him winningly. He swaggered across the floor to meet with Candy, who took his arm in a friendly manner and they ascended the staircase to her upper rooms.

Once out of Nate's sight, the pair walked along the corridor and entered Candy's suite of private rooms. They went in to find Hart and Letterman seated at a round table, upon which were two plates of sandwiches, a bottle of whiskey and four glasses. The room was well furnished to a high standard, with little regard for femininity; being beautifully appointed with good quality furniture, deep pile carpet and heavy drapes. It was almost masculine in its effect. Two further doors led off to Candy's private rooms.

"Good. Now we're all here," Candy said immediately dropping her cute appealing pose of the saloon floor and unceremoniously disengaging herself from Jackson, all pretense of intimacy vanishing. "Gentlemen, we have much to discuss and consider.

"You may not have heard, Charles, but earlier this evening the new marshal beat McCrae to a pulp and burnt down his entire saloon."

Letterman knew already, but Jackson and Hart looked aghast.

"Him, that young cowboy beat McCrae? I'd never have believed it. Must have been a helluva fight."

"It was. With the Barrel gone it means more of the boys need places to stay. Many have been posted to leave town by the marshal. Also, the Yateses are still on their ranch. Again, the marshal saw them and helped set them up again. And, Charles, three of your men who came in to finally scare them off are in jail for assault and are to be tried and charged."

"Who is this new marshal? Some hardcase brought in? I thought it would all collapse once Gorringe got shot and Lewis would be running the show," Jackson asked.

"His name is Nate Carlton. Cattleman and trail boss, you hear of the Syndicate herds? He brought one up last year and broke Brannigan's bunch wide open when he tried to cut it. Same happened in Dodge at the pens this year. A gun hung reputation hunter and his friends tried to cut Carlton's herd. Two are now dead. Stories come across of shootings in the south too; and he faced down Randall of the DR Connected. Took what was owing to him and thrashed him.

"This boy won't back off."

"Now it figures," Jackson muttered. "This marshal called in at the mines. He's hooked up with McKenzie, they're going to ship the ore I hear, all the way to Denver."

"When? I knew nothing of this already," Letterman asked, peaked that there was something about which he did not know.

"Oh, I have my ways," Jackson said. "Going to happen in the next week or so. They're gonna arm the stage and the marshal is going to ride along. Sounds like the time he's

155

gonna get shot. We'll kill two birds with one stone. Get the gold and kill him. Then take over the land and the mines."

"Wait," Candy cut in sharply. "When are they shipping it? Do we know the route?"

"I don't know the exact day, but we'll keep an eye on the Wells Fargo office and now that we own the telegraph office as well, nothing will get past us. Your man still holding back that telegram about the U.S. Marshal?"

"He is. But let's get back to the stage. They can only go one way north, initially, anyway," Letterman confirmed.

"Won't be a problem. My boys will keep a look out both ways. One trail is longer, but mebbe safer, the other shorter but more exposed. We won't hit 'em until the end of the first, or second day. It's three days' travel by stage. They'll be tired and happy, just waiting to be jumped. You'll see."

"Good. Then while the marshal is away, we'll move in again on Yates's place and maybe Farnham. But Yate's first, he doesn't know what he's sitting on. No one does," Candy ordered. "We need those mines and if the ore is lost, their cash will stop. We need complete control to offer to the railroad land and make the mines ours."

Letterman spoke up: "I'm working on that back east. My nephew is courting the railroad. He has them eating out of his hand. But as soon as the proposals become public the lid will blow off. Everyone anticipates them pushing further east and south, but no one knows exactly how or where."

"There is still the ranch land, too. It's good land and the more we control the fewer we are up against," Hart injected. "The potential is lucrative, army contracts; supplying the towns; and shipping east if the railroad comes in."

Making of a Lawman

Each party nodded around the table. "But I'm grateful to you for the information about Carlton. My daughter has been mooning over him in calf love. With this and after the fight, I will finally be able to kill that dead," he muttered looking into his whiskey glass.

Candy smiled; she could see why Isobel was smitten. The marshal was a fine young man and she had tried to warn him off. Still there was no sentiment where business was concerned and she needed to gain control, too much was at stake.

"Let's keep on track, gentlemen. We need more plans here," she concluded.

Chapter Sixteen

Nate had continued on his rounds, and made it back to the marshal's office. He found a meal brought round by Kim and some fresh coffee for which he was grateful. The next day he rose stiff as a board, but when he tried his fingers he found that he could flex them with ease. He praised Cal and his horse liniment, trying first for his Navy Colt. There was a bit of stiffness but he could work the trigger easily enough. He buckled on his gun belt, flipped the Colt in place and drew. Not as fast as normal, not the same blinding speed where the gun seemed to jump up to meet his hand, but it would do, the slight stiffness slowing him down, both from his shoulders and his hands.

"Not good, but better than I had expected," he muttered to himself.

"Looks pretty damned fast to me. Where'd you learn to use a gun like that?" Morg asked.

"Hmm, that's slow, and the man who taught me, would

be laughing at me and telling me to wake up!" Nate smiled in response.

"Wow, I'd like to see him in action."

"So would I. Sadly he was shot in the back down in South Carolina in a card game. But I got the man who did it," Nate responded as calmly as he could. "Now, it's Saturday so we're going to be busy. Cowhands coming into town and miners with pay in their pockets. I saw two more of the bad saloons closed and packed up last night. Their names were on the list. We're getting there," Nate added.

"We are. What are we doin' today?"

"Well, we'll get these yahoos loose and out of town. Check on some others and clean as much up as we can before dark and everyone gets lickered up. The Hart's will be in today and I want to see Isobel. I saw her father last night entering the Northern Star and meeting with his banker, Letterman and a chap called Jackson. Does that name mean anything to you? Tall, dark hatchet face, mean looking?"

"Stu Jackson? If it's him, he hails from Montana, bad man to cross. Supposed to have killed a few men and held up stages. No one ever caught him at it. Gun for hire and poison mean with a pistol."

"Now what would he be doing mixing with Hart and Letterman? And Candy? Or maybe they were just meeting privately at the Northern Star. I like this less and less the more I know.

"Come on let's send these jailbirds on their way."

With which they unshackled the four gun hands from the previous evening, saw them to the livery stable and made sure they rode out of town. Two more gambling dens had closed and Nate admired the smoking ruins of the Barrel saloon noting that no other premises had burned down. All in all, a good night's work he reflected. Then he saw a surrey come gamboling along the main street, a girl holding the ribbons and doing a fine job. Seeing him as the distance closed, she gently eased the horses to a walk to stop in front of him. A cowhand was seated next to her and scowling down at him was one of the two men he had shown off the Yates's ranch.

She took his hand to jump down. "Oh, Nate. I hear that you're the new marshal. Why?" were her first words.

"And a lovely good morning to you too, Isobel." He smiled down at her.

She laughed. "Oh, I'm sorry but I was bursting to talk to you and oh dear, where are my manners? And what happened to you face, it's all bruised?"

"Come on. Let me buy you a cup of coffee and I'll tell you all."

"Oh, I'd like that. Curly, take the surrey and hitch it by the store. I'll be along later."

"Yes, ma'am. Marshal, when do I gets our rifles back?" he barked.

"Go to the jail, the deputy is there, he'll hand 'em over. But no trouble, I warn you."

"Huh, sounds like you got enough already." And with that he took the ribbons and set off for the jail.

"What did he mean?" Isobel asked turning back to Nate.

"Ah, a rather long story, I fear. Let me tell you all over coffee," Nate responded. At times, especially when talking with Isobel, he reverted to his English mode of speech. He brooked no argument and gently took her arm, leading her to the nearby café.

It was half an hour later when he finished his explanation, throughout which she had interrupted and asked questions, her face aghast.

"So you are goin' through with all this, being a marshal and cleaning up the town. Why?" she asked stunned.

"Because as I explained, I feel obligated to do so. I feel responsible for not being there to save Clem and letting Marshal Gorringe down. Now I'm in, I won't give up until I have resolved it all and left the valley safe."

"And if that means crossing the Circle?"

"Why should it?" he asked blandly. "Those cowhands out the Yates's place said it was not your father who issued the orders. So he is in the clear as far as I can see," he finished gently, mentioning nothing of seeing him in town the previous evening.

"Yes, but if he wasn't, would you arrest him?"

"Isobel, what is this? I've said nothing about your father or anything to do with him. Why are you looking for trouble, where there is none?"

"Because I've heard rumors, gossip about the ranch, about oh, I don't know ... about you if you must know. Riding roughshod over everyone and now this fight with that saloon owner, even if he was a brute. It worries me and I don't want to see you hurt or worse."

"Trust me, neither do I, and as soon as the marshal is back on his feet again, I'm going to hand the reins over to him again and good riddance."

"And what if you get into more gun and fist fights?"

"Well, I'm marshal now. So I have the law on my side, more than most in this town," he said expansively, unsure of her seeming resentment.

"I see, but take care, Nate, and no guns in the night. I'd hate you to get shot or kill someone again. It all seems so brutal and unnecessary."

"Someone has to uphold the law and if I don't then anarchy will rule, with only the strong running roughshod over the weak. Would you really want that?"

Her lips pouted and she looked up under lowered lids: "I suppose not, but even so... Oh, I don't know. I care for you and don't want to see you hurt or changed, which would be worse."

"I know, I know," he said, gently clasping her hand. "Now I have to get on with my duties. I have to go to the mines and see McKenzie." He then fished a little, hating himself for it. "Is you father with you, are you seeing him for lunch?"

"No. He came in last night and stayed with his banker Mister Letterman and then he's taking me for lunch."

"That's a pity. It would have been nice to spend more time together."

"I'd like that. Can you come out to the ranch, maybe we could go for a drive and a picnic?" she encouraged.

They agreed upon a day and she left with a smile and a wave, though Nate's mind was far from easy at their words and parting.

He then headed for the jail and asked Morg to do something strange. "Morg, I've been thinking and I'm not sure I trust anyone now, especially with that new telegraph office opening. Any news coming in or out is supervised and open to abuse.

"I want you to go across to the key operator and say that he has been asked to report to his boss at the bank. Just see what he says. I'll be waiting to slip in as soon as he leaves, because I believe that he will."

Morg raised an eyebrow, but did as he was bid.

As Nate suspected the operator took off his eyeshade, left the office being guarded by Morg and hurried across the street heading in the direction of the bank at the far end in the area of business. Nate slipped in and quickly began sending a message to the next station, receiving confirmation of receipt. He wrote nothing down on the pad and tapped away from memory.

"Say, where'd you learn to do that?" asked a surprised Morg.

"In the war, we used morse code a lot and as someone who could read and write well, I was often chosen to send and decode messages. Now, keep an eye on that door. Let me know if the operator is returning." At which Morg stood outside leaning easily against the store front.

"Here he comes, doesn't look happy."

"Right before he gets within hailing distance, move off, wave to him and make yourself scarce."

"Will do."

He saw Morg wave and shift off down the street, with the operator huffing and puffing, a frown on his creased face. Nate heard him muttering to himself from the side window having let himself out through the back door. He was annoyed that he had not received a reply in time, but had hopefully covered his tracks.

Nate turned the corner and pushed open the door. "Morning. I wonder if you could help?"

"Sure, marshal. What can I do for you?"

"Well, I sent a telegram when I first got to town days ago and I haven't heard a dickie bird since. No messages for me are there?" he said innocently.

"No, sir, not that I've seen, but if one arrives I'll be sure to pass it straight along. Say, if you see that young deputy, tell him he got his wires crossed. Mr. Letterman didn't want to see me at all."

"Well, I don't know anything about that, but I will certainly pass the message on."

"Hopefully my response will arrive soon. Good morning to you," Nate said, tipping his hat as he left a smile on his face.

His next stop was at the Wells Fargo office and here he made it very obvious where he was going. He took his time so all would see, driving speculation about an ore shipment. He met with the office manager, a lady called Sheila Winn, whose husband also was the driver.

"Howdy, ma'am, I'm Marshal Nate Carlton. I wonder if you and your husband can help me."

"Morning, marshal, I know who you are. I'm Sheila Winn. I'll fetch my husband, please have a seat."

Nate thanked her, but stayed standing as she went to fetch her husband. The pair returned a few minutes later. Her husband was of medium height, in his early thirties, with a strong handshake brought on from hard work and handling the ribbons.

"Howdy, marshal, good to meet you. You're doing some grand work, if a might controversial." He smiled as Nate met his grip with a firm response.

"Well, I think I'll take that as a compliment but it had to be done. We'll doubtless get the town sorted soon and make it a lot safer all round. To which, I have a proposition for you and would be pleased if you'd hear me out?"

They both nodded, their faces giving nothing away and non-committal, so Nate continued: "I wanted to talk with you and your wife. I understand that you won't make a run for fear of getting held up and shot to pieces, which I have every sympathy for your sentiments. However, I have a plan that might just draw out the holdup gang and keep you and your shotgun guard safe at the same time. Would you care to hear it?"

"Go on, marshal, we're listening. But before you go any further let me fetch Jim Oates as he's the guard and he'll doubtless want to hear this."

Sheila disappeared in a bustle of skirts whilst Al Winn poured him a cup of coffee that was strong enough to take the bark off an oak tree. He winced but took another sip, setting it down carefully and talked of general matters concerning the stage runs, wanting to get a better feel for what he was proposing.

A few minutes later Sheila Winn returned with a tall lean man in tow. He had a whipcord strength about him and an inner toughness. He had a low-slung Colt at his hip, untied but a piece of pigging thong hung loose down his leg. The man looked capable and unlikely to be fazed by any form of action.

"I recognize you, marshal. I saw you in the street last night. Fine piece of work taking out McCrae. Mind, you didn't have it all your own way and I was concerned for you at one point, I'll admit."

"I have to admit he had me worried for a while too, and I'm more than a tad stiff this morning. But it sent a clear message to others and already some of the bad elements have left town. But not all, and some hang out along the trail which brings me to why I'm here. I want to run an ore shipment and advertise that you'll be shipping it."

"As you said, marshal, we won't run a trip like that. Too risky and Wells Fargo will back me."

"Let me explain what I have in mind and then see if you're still against it. If you are, we'll say no more and I'll try and find another way," Nate offered.

They sat down in a rear office and Nate outlined what he had in mind.

"Very interesting idea," Al muttered rubbing his stubbly chin. "And you think they'll hit later in the day?"

"Well, that is the part that I can't guarantee. But putting myself in their place, they would want to be sure which trail you are taking. The fork happens about half a day's ride up north. Before that point, I think it's too close to town, easy to ride back, get help or just alert the miners. It all adds to the risk and by that time in the normal course of events you and the guard would be relaxed, pulling into the first way station for a change of horses.

"You'd be thinking that you got so far and well away

from the town and no one is going to try anything. If they do go for the stage before that, I'd be surprised, and if I'm honest, yes, we'd have a fight on our hands. But depending on the odds, I'd say we run away, move back let them take what they want and then trail them. But I don't think it will come to that." Nate finished summing up what he had explained.

"Pretty sneaky, marshal, I'll give you that. Might work though, might just work," Oates offered. "Well if you are willing, I'm game, Al."

"Sheila?" he asked of his wife.

"It's a clever plan and well thought out. It mitigates the danger to us and I would love to see their faces if it works as you plan, marshal. But ultimately it rests with you Al."

Al thought for a moment. "OK, Marshal, we're in. Let me know the time and place and give me some notice and we'll make a lot of noise and let things slip, sneaky like, as you planned."

"That's good. We might just put one over on them. Now I have other people to meet and make more arrangements. I'll be back to see you soon once I hopefully receive the telegram confirming the answer to my questions. Thank you for the coffee, ma'am," Nate said as he tipped his hat and smiled leaving the Wells Fargo office.

Chapter Seventeen

Two days' passed and still Nate heard nothing. He had visited the mines again and the Yates's place to make arrangements and see that the family remained unharmed.

Half of the worst elements had left Langtonville. Gaps were now seen with empty buildings or tents where short term operations had been previously. The nights were quieter with only two more killings down alleys and one more arrest. The town was seemingly becoming tamer. Yet Nate suspected it was a false dawn, with the worst yet to come.

On the third day he headed to the telegraph office and was rewarded with a smile from the key operator. "Ah, Marshal. I was just about to come and see you when I had a moment. There is a new telegram for you. Here we are, and that'll be a dollar fifty five."

"Thank you." Nate took the folded message: N CARLTON NOTED AND AGREE STOP WILL

EXPECT YOU ON 18TH AT 4.30 PM STOP SUBJECT TO TRAIN ON TIME STOP RR STOP

"Oh, excellent news. Aunt Roberta latterly arrived from England is arriving in Denver on the eighteenth subject to the trains running on time, of course." He gave a sublime smile to the operator and paid him his fee.

"Any reply?" he asked.

"No, that's fine. She will doubtless be traveling and I wouldn't know where to send it." He left with a spring in his step and doubled back when out of sight to see the operator scurry away to the bank.

The man entered through the front door in a hurry asking the teller to allow him through or fetch Letterman. He was shown through to Letterman's office. The tall, well set up banker smoothed back his mane of greying hair with one hand, then pulled down at his satin waistcoat and turned to face the operator, calm and unruffled, his handsome head slightly tilted in a questioning manner. "Well?"

"The marshal just received a telegram and as you asked for anything unusual or interesting, I copied it." He handed the copy over. "Says his Aunt Roberta is over from England and he's going to meet her from the train at Denver on the eighteenth."

Letterman read the note. "He told you the bit about meeting his aunt?"

"He did. Seemed very happy to be meeting with her again."

"Did he send a reply?"

"No. Said she'd be traveling, so he'd just meet her there."

"The eighteenth? Well Denver is three days' ride, even by

stagecoach. Very good, you've done well already. I'll let you know if I need to send a telegram."

Then once by himself, Letterman gathered that the stage and probably Carlton would be leaving in a day's time.

Nate smiled to himself, pleased with the events as he watched Letterman leave and walk across the street to the Northern Star saloon. A few minutes later he saw from his vantage point, one of the gunmen leave in a hurry, mount his horse and ride north out of town. Nate nodded to himself, satisfied with the result and slipped away back to the jail.

Nate rode out later that day to the mines to go over the final arrangements for what he had planned with McKenzie. Again underlying that he wanted not a word of their conversation or plans to be discussed with anyone else, even those he trusted.

On the fourteenth of June, it was becoming known about town that a stage run was being made to Denver and passengers were to be restricted, if at all, as ore was being transported and weight was an issue. It was noted in the gazette that both Nate Carlton and the deputy Morg Newly would be riding shotgun to ensure its safe passage to Denver.

"That'll put some of the hold-up artists off trying, but if'n that gang up to the north is as strong as you say with Jackson running ramrod on it, they'll try sure a shootin'," Morg declared.

"That is exactly what I'm counting on. I just pray that they don't try it until after the fork in the trail when we're well clear of the town. The stage is advertised as leaving at nine in the morning on the fifteenth. We'll see if they take the bait or not."

Later that day a wagon came into town with outriders of miners, rifles drawn and looking mean and menacing, guarding the load. McKenzie was at its head, alert and rifle by his side in readiness. It pulled up outside the Wells Fargo office, where double doors were swung open and the wagon pulled inside. The tarp was pulled back by two of the miners and strong wooden boxes locked with stout padlocks were revealed.

"We've refined the ore as much as we can and a lot of gold dust is bagged and boxed, too," McKenzie offered in a loud voice, audible to any who may be eavesdropping outside or passing to building.

A silent figure hung back in the side alley, listening at the window, pleased with this intelligence and sneaked off before he could be recognized or seen, slipping away to enter the Northern Star saloon by the rear door. He went into the saloon and sought out Candy, speaking with her in private.

That evening the town turned wild again, with shootings at one of the far saloons. A man ran from that end of town to the marshal's office. "Marshal," he said breathlessly, "there's trouble at Dillon's place. Two men on the loose, angry at losin' at cards. They've got the whole place under guns, threatening to shoot it up or burn it down if'n they don't get their money back. They're primed for bear and shot two bouncers who tried to stop 'em."

"I'll be along. Go back now and tell Dillon not to do anything, keep calm. I'll be there it a minute."

The man nodded, pleased with the information and ran out.

"You know it's a setup, don't you?" This from Marshal

Gorringe who had insisted on hobbling to the jail. His leg much better, but still walking with a crutch.

"I do," Nate answered. "It's what I expected. The miners looked to leave town but six of 'em slipped back. They're all there now waiting, eager to defend the station. If anyone tries for the ore they'll get more than they bargained for. This will be a ploy to get me down there, I know. But it won't go how they planned. Morg, this is what we'll do."

Two minutes later they both left the jail, Morg from the front door, Nate from the rear.

Morg walked down the street in the shadows of the sidewalk, looking at his pocket watch. When three minutes had passed he went past Dillon's saloon, then stopped abruptly. His one hand held the shotgun on a sling over his right shoulder, the other held a heavy wooden bucket used for slopping out the cells. At exactly five minutes after he left the jail, he swung the bucket around letting go as it smashed into the saloon window. He ducked low and to the side, rewarded with a fusillade of shots two seconds after the glass smashed. Then silence and stillness prevailed. Then he heard Nate's voice.

Nate stood just inside the back door of the saloon having entered from the rear alley. A gunman was pushed forward as he walked into the main saloon, his hands raised and with an empty holster. His presence and resistance to Nate's entry reaffirmed more than ever that this was a setup.

"Alright, boys, drop the guns!" Nate ordered, a rifle resting on the gunman's shoulder, his whole body obscured by the man's torso.

"Do what he says, Joe!" the gunny shouted into the silence as all eyes turned towards Nate.

"I also bet you boys are out of bullets. Drop 'em now!" With each second he moved further forward now level with the nearest table. "You men, move. I want you in front of me. Get over there where I can shoot you easily or you leave, your choice."

The drinkers at the nearest tables got up hurriedly and moved away making for the bar or within the deeper part of the saloon out of the firing line. "Come on in now, Morg. I have it covered," he shouted.

The two men who had been shooting up the place looked suddenly sober, the owlish expressions disappearing with the realisation that their play had been spoiled.

Morg appeared at the double doors, shotgun ready and aimed low. No one wanted to argue with a shotgun in a confined space.

"You!" Nate pointed at the man who had run to the jail. "You set me up!"

"No, marshal, you got it all wrong," he pleaded.

"Really? Then where are the two bouncers who were shot?"

He looked at Dillon, who was behind the bar calmly standing with a cheroot hanging from the corner of his mouth. He took a draw and went to remove it in a seemingly innocent gesture, bringing his hand up and then down. "Marshal, you have this all wrong you see..." He began speaking gently, agreeably, then the hand flashed down to the bar edge, bringing up a Webley Bulldog revolver. It spat flame as Nate's rifle fired in response. Never the most accurate handgun when fired by instinctive alignment, the bullet took the gunny in the chest, Nate's own shot catching Dillon in the shoulder sending him spinning back into the bottles at the back of the bar.

Then the blast of a shotgun sounded from the front of the saloon. The two gunmen tried to draw and Morg pulled the trigger on one barrel of the weapon as the cylinder span lining up another. The gunny was flung into the air, almost cut in two by the blast at close range, his waist a bloody mess. His partner took some pellets but not enough to stop him as Nate pushed his protective gunman forward, levering a shell in one handed, swinging the rifle up and around then leveled the Winchester one handed to put a bullet in him. The gunman sprawled on the floor. Nate stood ready, Winchester in both hands, sweeping the room.

Morg called out, "Nate, up!"

A gunman on the balcony was leveling a pistol. Nate dropped too late burned in the shoulder by a bullet. He returned fire and caught the gunny dead center with the greater accuracy of the rifle, as the man toppled backwards, gut shot. No one else dared move.

"Dillon," he said, "you're finished. I want you out by tomorrow or I'll smash this place up and burn you in it. Hear me?" He turned as he spat the words facing the saloon owner.

"You wouldn't dare. This is in the middle of the town, not like McCrae's. Why, the town would go up in flames." He snarled in defiance, a hand held to his wounded shoulder.

"Just you try me," Nate replied as a crimson patch spread over the left shoulder of his shirt. "Close it now!" At which he moved over to the wall where a fancy oil lamp was hanging, matching many that illuminated the saloon along the walls.

Nate drew his Colt and placed the barrel to target the lamp. "Out everyone now!" he ordered. There was a stampede as the saloon emptied out onto the street just as shots were heard from down at the Wells Fargo office.

"Morg, this way, not on the street, too exposed in the dark," Nate shouted.

Morg ran to the back of the saloon and with Nate covering him they ducked in the cover of darkness, running down the back alley to get to the Wells Fargo office. They halted just before the last building to see a fire fight in process before them, as various guns threw flame into the night. The miners were putting up a spirited defence, returning fire from within the depot. Yet they were going to be overwhelmed soon as the outlaws pressed inwards running from cover to cover.

"Morg," he said above the gunfire, "you cover me to that trough. Don't shoot unless you have to. Then stay low and as soon as you see me in cover, let 'em have it."

In the shadowed light Morg nodded, his throat dry, adrenaline coursing through his body. "Will do." With that he broke the Colt revolving shotgun slipped in another shell and readied himself.

Nate, keeping low, made it to the wooden water trough half way between the wall of the depot and the street. Once dropping down he cursed as the wound on his shoulder opened again with a stinging sensation as sweat entered the gouged bullet track.

Assured that Morg was ready he leveled his rifle at where he had last seen a shot fired and as soon as it reappeared he squeezed the trigger. A cry sounded as a dark figure was thrown up to lie flat on the hard packed ground.

Then a shotgun blasted, sounding loud in the night, reverberating off the walls of the buildings. Another figure turned at the sound letting loose with a shot aimed at Morg's position. Nate squeezed another shot and he fell back struck in the chest. *Like shooting fish in a barrel*, he thought, as more directed their fire away from the depot to face the new attack. Twice more the rifle and shotgun sounded and three more men fell dead under the storm of lead.

"It's Marshal Nate Carlton here. Throw down your guns and surrender!"

A muffled voice shouted to leave and figures scurried away in the dark. The attack from the street stopped as horses' hooves were heard galloping into the night. And as quickly as it had started, it ceased. Townsmen raised from their beds tentatively approached, shouting their names as they did so.

Among them was Mayor Roberts. "Marshal, you there? Don't shoot it's Mayor Roberts," he called out.

"Come ahead, mayor, we're all clear. How you boys doing in the depot?" he shouted out, clearly identifying his position.

"One dead from a ricochet, one wounded," came McKenzie's distinctive voice.

The door to the depot opened and there he stood, rifle still at the ready. "Somebody get a doctor," he called as the townsmen approached.

Nate and Morg surveyed the scene of carnage. Five bodies lay sprawled on the ground and a blood trail showed where a sixth had been wounded. Torches displayed the grizzly tally, not revealing the full horror of the bloody corpses.

"Marshal, six more bodies!" the mayor declared, Judge Raybold at his side. "When will this end, Carlton? There has been carnage since you took office. You vowed to clean up the town, not start a war."

"Agreed," Raybold added. "Gone too far."

Then McKenzie's Scottish burr cut into the night: "Listen you two old goats, the laddie didna ask these owlhoots to attack us, we were prepared, thanks to him. Otherwise all our ore would be gone and you the poorer for it. I bet there's not an innocent man lying out there to count the cost, so back off the lad, he did well."

The two men looked slightly shamed face and went off into the night muttering as the doctor arrived carrying his case, bustling into the depot to attend the wounded miner.

McKenzie said: "Thanks to you we're all safe and secure." He placed a huge paw upon Nate's shoulder, not realizing he was wounded. Nate cried out in pain. "Sorry, laddie. I didna ken you were shot."

Nate laughed it off, but McKenzie steered him to the doctor inside the depot as a white faced, but stoic Sheila Winn appeared down the stairs from their rooms above, still carrying a rifle, her husband by her side.

"You're hurt, marshal," she declared, concern in her voice.

"It's nothing but a scratch, ma'am. It won't stop me for tomorrow, rest assured."

Yet she did not heed his response. Moving forward she put down the rifle and fetched hot water to bathe the wound before the doctor had finished tending the seriously wounded miner.

Chapter Eighteen

The following morning before dawn, Nate woke, stiff in the shoulder, but able to flex properly. He saw Morg staring at him over a cup of coffee.

"You're up early, couldn't you sleep?"

"No," he said shaking his head. "Bad dreams of men dying, blown apart from a shotgun. The images will stay with me forever, I guess."

"It's never easy to face it, especially up close. It was terrible in the war seeing trenches filled with dead, mutilated bodies caused by gunshots. It never goes away but it does fade," he assured Morg.

"Yea, I hope so. Glad I was too young to serve in the war."

They washed, dressed, checked their armaments and then left by the early dawn light, walking along the empty sidewalk.

"You can bet that someone will be watching the depot,

even now, I reckon," Nate said out of the corner of his mouth.

"Sure to be."

They knocked lightly on the side door to the depot seeing all the rough grazes and scrapes from the previous night's fight and were let in by Sheila Winn.

"Morning, you two, bright and early. Can I get you a coffee?"

"No thanks, ma'am. I'd like to be on our way, soon as we can," Nate answered, fearing the strength of her coffee more than any bullet.

Al and Jim appeared, all dressed and ready, keen to be away. Two saddle horses were tacked up and tethered to the rear of the stagecoach and the team were in harness and ready to go. Two of them stamped their feet in impatience, knowing they were soon to be off. It didn't take long. Al kissed his wife goodbye, then swung up onto the bench seat beside Jim, who had a shotgun in the boot and a rifle in his hand.

Nate and Morg pushed open the huge doors to the depot; Al kissed to the horses, flicked the ribbons and they pushed into the harness rolling the stage out into the street. Nate and Morg swung aboard with a final few words with Sheila Winn and then the stage rolled forward at a walk.

The sun was just coming up and Jim took off his hat, reset it against the shallow angled slanting rays, and admired the early morning view as the stage left the town, two hours ahead of schedule.

A man posted up on one of the balconies above the Northern Star, cursed and muttered. "Damn that man, don't he never sleep?" He slid down the front post, hit the ground softly and ran to the corral at the back where his horse was tethered. He had a way to go and important news to impart to Jackson.

After a mile the stage horses were pushed up into a steady ground eating lope as they leaned eagerly into the harness: the six horses, perfectly matched and running well, the two saddle horses behind, easily keeping pace.

"Well, we're out and running. Think we were spotted?" Morg asked.

"Sure to be; there'll be watchers along the way soon and my feeling is that one will be where the trail splits. It'll take time to get to the camp and warn Jackson that we are away. Then get him rousted out and on the trail. My best guess is a couple of hours at least, before he can make any attempt upon us. By which we'll have chosen a trail and the rest is up to good luck and a prayer."

Morg nodded calming his thoughts, ready expectantly for action.

It was two hours later that they hit the fork dividing for the two different trails. A flash of light flicked across the valley as they passed one of the huge sandstone buttes.

Jim called down into the coach. "Light up there, reckon they know which way we're goin'."

"Good, keep straight ahead, until we pass Cactus Mesa as agreed. Then after that bend in the valley we'll stop. Difficult to be seen there for about two hundred yards from the heights."

They carried on as planned and as they passed the heights and Cactus Mesa, Al slowed the horses that he had been driving sparingly. They got out, stretched their legs and loosened the pin in the offside wheel. "Still don't see why we need to actually do this," Al moaned. "Might break the damned wheel or an axle."

"Yes, but it needs to be legitimate and then they won't chase you as they'll think it was an accident. By the time they find out differently, you'll have a good head start and be well on the way home. Trust me, it's for the best."

They set off again at a slow pace, with a clear view now from the higher ground afforded to any watcher.

"Wheel's wobblin'!" Jim shouted from the top of the box. "Any minute now, slow it. Yep, here she goes!" The stagecoach lurched and slapped down on its axel. The speed was minimal when it happened and Al brought it to a controlled skidding halt.

Looking up, Nate saw a flash of a signal bouncing across the mesa tops. "Right let's go. Get saddles on the two stage horses, we'll lead the rest," he urged. It was the work of minutes to unharness and saddle the stage horses and with them all mounted astride, they abandoned the coach and its haul of secure boxes, heading back the way they had come.

Ten minutes after they had abandoned the stage, another group of riders appeared headed by Stu Jackson, who led them to the deserted stagecoach, where by the side stood the watcher who had come down the steep trail from the top of the mesa as soon as he had signaled and saw the others ride away. As the outlaws skidded to a halt in a cloud of dust Jackson came forward.

"Wheel came off, saw it happen." He laughed humorlessly. "Coach collapsed and they skedaddled off back to town. Couldn't take the ore with them, too heavy so it's all inside. Easy pickings all round, I'd say." He cackled.

Jackson stood down from the saddle, a grim smile on his face. "Shame, I wanted to have it out with that marshal, but he'll keep. Get the boxes of ore. Load it up on the horses, boys, stow them to the back of the saddles.

"You said some contained dust, Mike?"

"Yea, least ways that's what we heard at the depot."

"Right, we'll haul it off the trail into the hills and then break it open see what we've got. Tel will be there shortly with a wagon and we can use that to transport the heavy stuff. Looking at these boxes, why if they're full of good stuff, there could be hundreds of thousands of dollars' worth here.

"Come on, boys let's get to work," he ordered.

Further down the trail Nate and the others rode steadily for two hours. A few miles from the town they were met by the livery owner Cal and Sheila Winn who had been sat under a small copse of sycamores, with the horses swishing their tales against the flies.

"You made it!" she said with obvious relief.

"We sure did, honey. Fooled 'em just like Nate said." Al whooped.

"Yes, but we're not out of the woods yet. As soon as they realise that the boxes are full of nothing but dirt and rocks, they are going to come hunting us as angry as a swarm of hornets. So, I want you all back safely in town. Sheila, Cal, I appreciate this." Nate thanked them as he swapped horses to take the reins of Patch, who had been brought along. Morg jumped on his own saddle horse, a beautifully put together bay Morgan gelding, with a nice sloping shoulder and showing good bloodlines. They made their goodbyes and loped off at a fast canter in the direction of the mines, wasting no time.

An hour later they skirted to the north of the hills, coming in at the back on the eastern side where Nate had first ridden days before. They had cut through a huge side of a triangle, pushing the horses as fast as they could, knowing time was of the essence. They arrived breathless, the horses blowing hard to come up on the eastern side of the deep arroyo. Before their eyes stood three wagons, currently being loaded with boxes of ore from a train of pack mules that had made the shorter journey through the knoll where no wagons could be taken down the arduous steep trail of the arroyo to be unloaded onto the waiting wagons.

McKenzie was there supervising as was Yates and two of his neighbors who had supplied the wagons for hire. The money would be welcome by all and help them get a new start.

"Morning to you, laddie, your plan worked. We lost just one mule on the trail, fell and broke her leg; but we got all the ore and dust here. We're nearly finished loading now."

"Good to see you, McKenzie. So no hitches or trouble?" Nate asked fearing the worst and impatient to be off, knowing that time was eroding even as they spoke.

McKenzie pulled at his beard, a bad sign as Nate had come to know. "Well, I kept it quiet, as you said, as best I could, but once we got the mules together and started loading there was nothing I could do, word spread around the camp like wild fire. Yet they don't know what we plan, that I have kept secret, only that the stagecoach was a fake and the real ore is being taken by mule."

"You got the dynamite I asked for?"

"I have, though I'll not know why."

"Insurance. Where is Si? I thought he was one of your best blasters?"

"Well, that's the thing, he is. He is also missing; seemed to disappear along with one or two others just after we started packing the mules."

Nate cursed under his breath. "Then you'll come with us, McKenzie. I need someone I can trust."

"That I will. Allen here will look after the mines, he's one of the main shareholders." He indicated a shortish man as broad as he was tall, with big hands like shovels. Nate recognized him as being one of those in the party the previous night and knew he would stand fast.

"Allen, go back as soon as you can. They may still hit the mine thinking that we have left a haul behind. Be prepared; double the guards and put scouts up on those mesas above where we had the ambush that night."

"Will do. Don't worry, we'll be ready for them. Just get our gold to Denver and I'll be happy."

With all loaded, tarped and roped, the team of three wagons set off. Yates drove one as he knew the trail well and handled his team with ease. The others followed with McKenzie in the rear wagon keeping a lookout behind.

Nate made to join Yates on the bench seat and spoke finally to Morg. "Take care, Montana. Keep yourself safe back in town. Word will get out that we've pulled a fast one and they won't be happy. Watch out for being lured into a trap. Gorringe is getting better and listen to him, he is experienced, but take no chances. Hear me?"

"Yes, pappy!" Morg answered.

Nate smiled at him and jumped onto the bench waving back. "Right, let's roll!"

With a crack of a whip in the air, the lead wagon began to move forward as the team pushed into the harness. They started carefully down the trail that was a little known back track. Though flat, it wasn't used regularly and at times just wide enough for one wagon squeezing between rocky outcrops of red sandstone that had been weathered and blasted by wind, rain and man. Juniper clung to the walls, and small tumbleweeds sought to grip the soil of the trail. It was hot work, with stones and rocks strewn from recent slides across the soil. They pushed up the trail getting to high ground after four hours. The trail dropped down and came to a little spring that seeped into a natural rock basin before trickling away into a tiny stream. Here they stopped to water the horses.

"How far to Burlington from here?" Nate asked.

"About another hour, maybe an hour and half, if the trail holds and we get no problems. You sure the train will stop for us? It's just a tiny flee bitten hole with two cabins, a water tower and log store, and a saloon of sorts." Yates spat derisively.

"Well, I hope so or we are stuffed. The telegram was as clear as could be. They have got a loading ramp there you say?"

"Yea, allows the cattle to come off when they made an occasional stop to offload or get crops on from the farms. But it's usually people on board transporting. So, I hope you're right."

"So do I," Nate muttered. Then louder, "Come on, we need to be there by 4.30 and I don't want to be late."

They started rumbling along the trail again as it turned and meandered in a series of switchbacks that obscured the back route. Then as the ground rose again and the track straightened, McKenzie shouted from the rear wagon. "Nate, dust cloud behind, can't make it out but looks like a fair bunch of riders."

Nate got Yates to halt the wagon and he stood shielding his eyes against the sun. "Now we're in trouble. McKenzie, time for you to earn your keep. Up ahead about half a mile the draw narrows. I noticed this from the rise. Come on, now."

Yates cracked the whip and the team moved forward, lurching at better speed than he wanted. The trail widened then narrowed with smooth sandstone rising now steeply on either side. "Here, this will do. Let me off and pull forward for a good three hundred yards. It's going to get noisy and I don't want the horses spooked."

Nate jumped off holding his old Spencer and ran back as the third wagon drew level. "This will do, Tam. Let's get to work."

McKenzie needed no urging but jumped down, bringing a solid wooden box that he carried reverently before him. "This stuff has been jolting and is hot so we'll take great care.

I have a running fuse for both sides. You go to the left with Gus there and start setting them up."

The other miner who had been driving the wagon also had a box of dynamite and went to the left hand bank of red rock. He had a lump hammer and a cold chisel at his belt.

"Are you ready? There's a ledge above. I'll climb up while you fetch the rope from the wagon. Tie it well to the box and throw up to me as soon as I'm set," instructed Gus.

Nate nodded, carefully taking the box of blasting rods from him, placing it on the ground. He was nervous and sweat ran in rivulets down his face not from just the heat. One false move and he knew they would be blown to pieces.

Gus attacked the rock face with ease, seeming to find grips and footholds where there were none. Once up about twenty feet, he asked Nate to throw up the rope. Twice he failed in his nervousness, then Gus caught the coil on the third attempt, letting the end back down with enough slack to tie to the end of the box's rope handle.

"Easy now, just take the weight as I pull gently up," he encouraged as the box started to swing back and forth once it left Nate's hands. It caught with a knock on a jagged outcrop and both men held their breath, the silence sickening as they waited for the explosion that they would never hear. It swung free and Gus pulled at once clearing the snag. Once up, he untied the box and took out the sticks of dynamite, each linked by a fuse. He took one look from his elevated position to see that he could now make out specks of men and horses in the dust cloud.

"Damn, it's going to be close, they're moving," he shouted down.

Nate looked again at the approaching riders and went back to the wagon to fetch his Spencer carbine that he had left on the rear bed. "It won't be any good until about five hundred yards, but might deter them a little and slow them down," he said.

Gus was already chipping lodge holes for the sticks, chiseling into the soft sandstone. When he was ready, he shouted across to McKenzie: "Are you ready, Tam?"

The other Scot shouted he needed one more minute, as the other wagon driver who had been helping him looked up anxiously. He ordered him to get to the wagon and be ready to move it forward to safety. Nate did the same for McKenzie's wagon, but hesitated. He knelt down by a red boulder and pushed up the rear ladder sight on his weapon, adjusting to the maximum range, loaded a round, pulled back the hammer to full cock, sighted a target of a piece of prominent rock about five hundred yards away by his estimate, shouted to warn the others what he intended to do, held his breath, took careful aim, resting his carbine against the rock and squeezed the trigger. He missed. He took aim again reckoning that it had pulled about six inches to the left and two inches high. He tried again, this time much closer. He made adjustments and was rewarded with a puff of smoke nearly where he was aiming for.

"That'll do," he muttered to himself, levering another round into the breach and setting the hammer to half cock.

McKenzie shouted he was ready. And both men gave the thumbs up sign, struck their matches, made sure that the wire was fizzing away and scrabbled down the rock face as fast as they could.

Gus slipped the last four feet landing hard. He cursed at the pain in his ankle and made to get up hobbling, eyeing the approaching riders, now at full gallop and closing fast.

Nate ran forward helping him with an arm across his shoulder, dropping him at the forward wagon whilst McKenzie jumped up and took the ribbons for the third.

"Get up, laddie!" he ordered.

"No! It's too close, how long 'til it blows?"

"A minute maybe, give or take."

"Go then, get out of here. They're too close I need to dissuade them," Nate shouted and ran back to the rock with his Spencer.

McKenzie tried to shout, but Nate waved him away and with regret he whipped the horses who pulled with pleasure, keen to be away from the shots and the third wagon drove away.

Nate now looked into the distance and saw they were within six or seven hundred yards and coming fast, bunched down the narrow trail. He elevated the Spencer and squeezed off a shot, allowing for the vagaries of the distance. It must have buzzed by someone's head, for the man ducked, and others began to pull their rifles from the saddle boots, causing their pace to slacken a little.

Four left then I'm done, he thought, counting his rounds from the seven cartridge loading tube. He had no more tubes, the box with more being on the seat of the first wagon and he knew that he would never get a chance to reload a tube in time. He squeezed off another shot, this time emptying a saddle.

The riders pulled up, returning fire now, a volley of shots

pinging and whining around his position. Nate reckoned thirty seconds had gone if not more. He risked one more shot taking another man, flinging him sideways and now lead was being returned in earnest, with ricochets bouncing around the valley. "Time to go, Nate, old chap," he muttered and jumped back into a crouching run.

Luckily the riders had not dismounted and the horses provided a poor platform at this extreme range. One man now dropped, adjusting his sights and others followed suit. It gave Nate just enough time to get about fifty yards further away, zig zagging as he went expecting a slug to take him in the back at any moment. But every yard extended the range and most outlaws had only Winchesters or Henry .44s which were disadvantaged compared to the Spencer's bigger load and range.

Then the roar of the exploding powder caught his ears, just as he dropped into a cleft in the rock, before the percussive shock wave reached him, followed by a hail of debris loosed into the air. Then a second later a further explosion rocked the valley, closer this time on his side of the trail, the ground shaking and reverberating like a God of old roaring in anger. Choking dust filled the air and shaken by the force, Nate pulled up his silk bandana to cover his nose and mouth, coughing as he did so. His ears rang, but no blood came and he could still hear well enough to sense the cries of pain and anger from the outlaws on the other side of the now blocked trail. Nate emerged from his sanctuary to see a wall of red sandstone about thirty or forty feet high, completely blocking the trail. He took no time to admire their handiwork but ran as fast as he could, down the narrow trail to a waiting wagon, driven by McKenzie.

"We did it!" He whooped. "They'll not get through that in a hurry and it'll be deadly to climb even without horses." Then his thoughts turned to Nate. "Are you alright, laddie?"

"Ha, well that's a matter of opinion." He gasped. "My head hurts, my ears are ringing, my throat is clogged and all I can smell is sulphur. But yes, I'm fine and dandy. Now, let's get the hell out of here, we've a train to catch."

Chapter Nineteen

They made the journey to Burlington with minutes to spare. The train stopped as planned and the conductor and guard were aware of the arrangements. The ore was loaded and there were two extra guards aboard, both well armed and ready. No rider could catch the train now before it arrived in Denver, but the railroad had taken extra measures given the value of its cargo.

Watching the train puff off into the distance, the men, minus McKenzie who was traveling with the haul to oversee the mine's interests in Denver, looked around feeling a little deflated now that all the action was over.

"Well, I don't know about you chaps," Nate said, "but I could do with a well earned beer."

They all agreed and made for the large main building which served as a store, bar and café of sorts. It was cool inside, and smelled of stale beer, leather and tobacco, but it served son-of-a-gun stew, with mashed potatoes and beans.

All the men tucked in with gusto, hungry after the events and the day's ride.

"What now, Nate?" Yates asked.

"Let's get outside and I'll explain," he said quietly. Then in a louder voice, "We'll head onto the Denver trail but in time to meet with McKenzie on his return ride in a day or so. I've arranged to meet him at Limon and we'll all ride back together, safety in numbers."

The others asked no more questions and carried on eating.

Once they had coffee and left, he gathered them together where no one could hear.

"I have no intention of staying at that flop house this night." He nodded at the rather rough looking rooming house tacked onto the store. I'd rather use the wagons for beds and my suggan than trust the sheets there. Also, we don't know if the outlaws managed to find a way round and are possibly waiting for us. They can figure out as well as we can where we might possibly travel back, especially if they think we traveled on the train to Denver and will be coming down the main trail. Now I've warned McKenzie about doing that, so he's going back on the train to Burlington and stopping off here tomorrow. I don't want him being robbed on the way.

"Right, Graham. You take the others back by the eastern trail you told me about. Skirt out north, then come back, one by one out of sight. I may be being too cautious but there were some mighty unsavory looking characters in the bar and I've no wish for them to know what we're doing.

"Tomorrow I'll wait a few miles north of the tracks until

I hear the train and then pick him up. We'll be a day or so behind you. All clear?"

"Sure thing. You sure are a suspicious fella," Gus said, shaking his head.

"Indeed, and that's why I'm still alive and the gold got through," Nate responded.

"Well, I'll take my hat off to you there, that's for sure. Now we'll do what you say and head out."

It was getting close to the end of the day and dusk was approaching. There was still enough light to be seen by two men from the trading post saloon. They watched the wagons leave over the tracks and head north and west in the direction of Denver. When lost to sight, one went to the railroad office, trying to get the agent there to open up and send a telegram.

The wagons circled back after a couple of miles when they were sure that they were not being followed and ended up east of the town where they made camp in a hollow, near a stream. Their fire smoke could not be easily seen, but as soon as they were ready to settle down, Nate insisted that they move on another mile and make a dry camp in a small copse, where the wagons were all but invisible, despite their protestations.

"My job is to get you and your wagons back alive and in one piece, and I don't want to be the one to face your wife, and children if I failed to do so, Graham."

This brought Yates up short, having not seen the consequences of his carelessness. "Fair enough, Nate. I take your point," he agreed somewhat mollified.

They settled down for the night, and once they seemed

asleep, Nate pulled out away from the camp, which was no hardship.

It was a dry night and he had spent many such occasions using the stars for a roof. To him it had all seemed too easy, despite being followed by the outlaws. No one had come and he spotted the telegraph office attached to the railway post. He dozed not sleeping well, wishing that Buck or Patches were here, but he'd left them to be tended at the Yates's ranch until he returned.

In the early hours of the morning he was woken by something in his subconscious. He became instantly alert, but did not open his eyes, using his hearing alone and sense of smell to alert him to any unknown presence. No man who used the trail slept soundly as in his own bed. There was always part of the brain that stayed awake, never allowing deep sleep unless injured or exhausted. Then he heard it, the slight crunch of a twig being rolled beneath a boot. Someone was trying to move quietly and failed. Then the swish of a branch. It was coming from a few feet to his right heading for the circle of the camp where the others slept.

There was no moon just a vague ambient light, that would show darker images of shadow. Then he caught the smell of stale cigarette smoke in the air. *Shouldn't have had a smoke, boys,* he thought.

Carefully he pulled back the top of his suggan, and raised his right hand that held his Navy Colt. It was not cocked, and that sound he knew would carry, alerting the bush-whackers. He pulled himself upright using his stomach muscles and waited, every sense alert. There it was, the swish of a branch; one man was to the left about five yards away.

Nate waited to get an exact location on the other, then he sensed rather than saw him, a vague shadow about fifteen yards out at his two o'clock. He cocked his gun as he spoke: "Hold it, boys. We got you covered, drop your-"

He never got any further, the nearest man span, lining his pistol. Nate dropped the hammer of his Colt, the gun bucked in his hand, and he threw himself sideways. Two shots came in response from the other side of the clearing, tugging at the material of his suggan as it was pierced by lead. He was now lying prone on his stomach. Nate threw three fast shots at the muzzle flashes, and was rewarded with a croaking cry, then the sound of a body hitting the ground.

The camp was now alive and above the chaos, he heard the man to his left wheeze in agony: "Don't shoot! You got me plumb center, I dropped my gun."

"Come easy, Graham, Gus. I think I got them all, but come easy."

"We're here, Nate," Gus answered. "What the hell? How'd you know?"

Nate didn't answer him but came forward to where he crouched by one of the would be assassins. The man was holding his stomach that was dark and slick with blood, his hand doing little to stop the flow.

"Oh, God, the pain! I feel as though my insides are on fire. Said it would be easy, just two farmers and a couple of miners. Nothing about a gunman. Is Al dead? Oh God..." He moaned again sweat breaking on his forehead at the pain. "Water, please, please."

Gus returned with a canteen and raised it gently to his lips. He coughed and spluttered.

"Who sent you?" Nate asked, suddenly angry that he had had to kill again, the job and the trip seemed to be costing him a lot.

"Banker name of Letterman in town. Wired him...told... us to...kill you... Stop you meeting with the other man and way lay him on way back... Easy job he said, two hundred dollars." He rasped and then was dead, eyes wide open seeing nothing.

"Two hundred dollars! Two more dead over that gold and two hundred dollars," Nate said shaking his head. "I shall be having words with Letterman when we return," he added harshly, a latent threat in his voice. "Right, we'll get these two buried and then you had best move fast as soon as it's light. The longer you are on the trail the more dangerous it is and these two gunnies will be expected to send a telegram." Then he grinned to himself. "In fact, they will."

A few hours later he was back in Burlington at the telegraph office.

"Howdy, what can I do for you?" the clerk asked.

"Morning. I'd like to send a telegram, please."

"Sure where to?"

"The telegraph office at Langtonville."

The clerk looked up, from under his bushy eyebrows: "Seems like a right popular place of late."

"How so?" Nate asked innocently.

"Never mind, I can't discuss company business like. What's the message and who is it to?"

"To go to a fella called Letterman, Moises Letterman. He's the owner of the Langtonville bank." Here the clerk raised an eyebrow but said nothing. "Message to read: ALL DONE STOP ON TO NEXT JOB STOP AL.

"Got that?" he asked.

The clerk replied he had and read it back to Nate to confirm. Nate agreed, paid the fee and waited until the message was sent.

He stepped outside to sit in a chair on the veranda and minutes later the key started tapping its tune again. The clerk came out: message reads: GOOD STOP LET ME KNOW STOP.

"That do you?"

"It will. Thank you," Nate replied, slipping the clerk a tip and went on his way to the wagon and crossed the tracks north of the railway stop to disappear from sight.

Chapter Twenty

Two days' later after picking up McKenzie he returned to the mines from the knoll, having picked up Patch from the Yates's ranch. Graham Yates was delighted. His house was coming on with the rebuilding and he was pleased with the extra dollars earned from the trip to the north. Nate and McKenzie had dropped down the steep track of the arroyo and up the other side to come into the mining camp from the east. He was tired and wanted a bath, some good food and a comfortable bed where he could sleep deeply without fear of being shot.

He looked skywards, rain was coming or he missed his guess.

"Aye," McKenzie agreed, "there'll be a storm as like. Get yourself back afore it breaks," he urged.

Nate agreed leaving the camp just as the first heavy spots of rain started to fall. On a whim he suddenly pulled in under some trees, off the trail, half way between the town and the mines, not wishing to add pneumonia to his troubles as the air took on a chill driving the band of water before it. He pulled out his yellow slicker unstrapping it off the saddle and with that action saved his life.

Settled in place, Nate rode out from under the trees just as the storm started to break. An instantaneous flash of lightning seared the darkened day and a rifle shot cracked through the air, the bullet thumping into him. The second shot followed from the back. Nate fell forward across the saddle horn, grabbing hard, kissing Patch into a gallop. To get away was his only thought, pointing the stallion the only way that was open-north.

Patch was rested and loved to run, yet cared for his master. He broke into a fast smooth gallop, sensing the urgency having heard the shots. He ran north of the mines, circling in on a narrow trail where Nate had traveled on the first day, coming in from the north west, behind the hills.

Nate, barely conscious, looked back, the rain stinging his eyes. He was being followed by two riders. Nate had to hang on. Patch seemed to know where he was going skirting the hills, then he had it, he was heading for the arroyo: could they get down and up in the rain? He would soon find out. Patch responded as Nate guided him to the top of the steep trail. Slithering in the fresh mud, Patch came to a halt, edging over onto the steep trail. The riders behind were gaining as they disappeared over the lip. Patch took his time, sure footed as he sat down on his haunches, each step smacked down hard as he tested the ground like a good trail horse. They made it to the bottom, where the stream was fast running and rising. Then through the pain and loss of blood,

Nate heard it, a roar and crash of rocks and debris being thrust through the deep cutting.

Patch needed no second urging. He splashed into the water, nature warning him of what was to come. He found the upper trail, where the higher part about six feet up had slid away. The Appaloosa stretched up, front hooves biting into the slippery trail mud, pushed and launched himself nearly unseating Nate, as he jumped past a break. Landing like a cat, he pushed up again in a series of lunges as the roar became louder. They were now some twenty feet off the bottom and the riders who pursued him were just making their way down the narrow trail. They were still unaware of the impending flood as they turned the last switchback. The air became wet with moisture, pushed before the tide of water. The men cried out in alarm, unable to turn on the narrow trail. One horse reared in fear, throwing its rider, who lost his balance, rifle in hand. His cry pierced the air, falling thirty feet or so to the valley base below.

The second man started to back his horse slowly and painfully upwards, whilst the fallen man rose awkwardly, his leg clearly broken. He hobbled to the trail, each step agony. Then round the bend in the arroyo the wall of water appeared, smashing all before it: a living, breathing entity, malevolent in its intent to destroy all before it. The luckless rider was swept away, his final screams drowned by the water.

Patch was now pulling up as fast as he could, reaching a natural ledge of sandstone. He stood quaking some fifty feet above the swirling water that was but a few feet below him. The ledge led inwards to a deep cleft and Nate urged him to follow. Patch whinnied in fear as the water rose, trying desperately to find a way to get out. The water crashed and roared, bringing with it tree trunks, boulders and other detritus, now level with the horse's knees. Swirling in eddies around his legs, the water reached the saddle and Nate in his rambling mind thought he would drown.

Then the level of the water seemed to only rise by a few inches, then it slowed, maintaining a steady level as uprooted bushes and logs floated by.

"We did it, Patch... We did it, boy... Thank you! By all that's holy, thank you," he muttered weakly as he praised the stallion, patting his soaking neck feebly. Gradually the water receded, until the pair were able to venture out onto on the ledge and continue rising up the trail, the rain bringing visibility down to only a few yards. He started to shiver with cold and saw that his slicker was streaked with rivulets of red and pink.

Patch made the top of the trail and pushed on seeming to know where he was going, fighting for high ground following the old game trail. At the two sandstone sentinels, almost hidden, he pushed through into the gap and entered the arcade of hazel. The rain was almost unable to penetrate the thick canopy and just dripped through in a continuous tattoo. Nate now unconscious, slipped from the saddle to lie in a heap on the floor. Patch stopped and looked down at his master, then proceeded to munch on the young juicy shoots of hazel above him.

Sometime later, Nate was woken as raindrops continually exploded on his eyes. He blinked and woke to find he was shivering almost uncontrollably. Everything felt so cold and numb, he could barely move. Patch still stood above him, waiting patiently. Nate wanted to sleep more, to stop and just sleep, to move would be painful he knew. If he just lay there it would go away and— *you'll die!* Part of his brain shouted at him and the deep seated will to live fought back.

He tried to move his right arm and found that he could, but as soon as he attempted to rise from the ground, red hot pain shot into his ribs, his head pounding with a glaring headache. *Got to get up or I'll die here*, were his only thoughts. He fought the pain, rolled onto his stomach and pushed himself up, grabbing at the stirrup leather with his right hand. He knelt upright, pants clinging to him, clammy and sopping. Then with great effort he finally stood. His head span, dizziness overtaking him and he threw up at his feet, his mouth full of bitter bile. He wiped his mouth with the back of his hand, spat and with great effort pulled himself into the saddle, his head blaring with agony.

They reached the end of the gallery of hazel trees, and pushed onto the narrow game trail and back into the rain heading upwards to finally reach the top of the mesa where he had camped that night, not so long ago. Patch walked to the copse as Nate slid from the saddle, weak and frozen from the wet clothes. He went to the cave where he had last slept, and with numb hands wrestled with the latigo strap, finally getting the pin out and pulled off Patch's saddle, dragging it into the shelter of the cave, leading the horse with him.

He found the stash of kindling and firewood he'd left from before. With fingers thick with cold, he managed to get a fire going, feeding it as the flames licked hungrily at the wood. When it was blazing and his hands had some feeling, Nate ventured forth to fetch more wood, pulling in a couple of dead falls that he lay by the blaze to dry and start burning. His wounds opened and bled again with the effort.

He then hobbled Patch, removing his bridle and left him to crop the grass. Every movement was a painful effort, but thankfully the rain had now reduced to a drizzle and he prayed that it would stop soon.

Exhausted and weak, he pulled off his boots and wet clothes, setting them to dry, dropped his head on the saddle for a pillow and was fast asleep, curled up in his suggan as near to the fire as he dare. He awoke hours later, as the fire had died down, the logs half burned through. He rose immediately, regretting it, the pain in his ribs severe and his head thumped.

Nate carefully pushed the logs closer, and the red embers caught, trickling with a small array of flames that grew as the fire caught hold again. Knowing he needed to treat his wounds, he pulled on his pants that were nearly dry. Thrusting a pistol into his belt, he shuffled out into the chilly night. It had stopped raining, but a wind had developed, bringing the temperature down. Using the birch trees nearby, Nate stripped off the bark with his clasp knife, fashioning a shallow bowl. From his canteen he filled it with water and set it to boil above the flames making sure none reached above the water line, so not to burn.

Shivering by the fire, he watched and within minutes the water boiled. He dipped his bandana in the water, cleaning first the wound at his ribs and then his head. This alone made him feel better and by the firelight saw that he had been lucky. The ribs were broken, evident by a deep groove but the bullet had missed his insides. An inch to the right and he would have been dead with a punctured lung or heart. His head wound was painful and had bled a great deal. This he bathed tentatively, washing away the sticky scab that hemorrhaged again, but at least he knew it was now clean.

Nate refilled his canteen from the trickle of water that emerged from the sandstone and drank greedily, slaking his thirst. Rejuvenated by the cool water, Nate fluttered his eyes closed and welcomed sleep's embrace.

Chapter Twenty-One

He woke in the morning, cold and shaking, a fever upon him. He was weak and hungry. The last food he had eaten was the day before; biscuits at the Yates's house over coffee. Finding some jerky in his saddle bags, Nate chewed on the strips, then drank deeply, rose and went to fetch more wood, shivering with fever as he did so.

With the fire once more burning well, he curled up in his suggan and slept again. He woke with a raving thirst to find that night had descended. With herbs that he had foraged he made a poultice with hot water and bathed his wounds again, tying his shredded shirt around his ribs to hold it in place. He had barely completed the task when, too exhausted, he fell asleep.

The next morning he awoke with his fever broken but feeling sick and frail and in need of some food. He pushed his gun into his belt and went to search for Patch, who had wandered off, grazing as he went, leaving a trail of cropped grass.

The sun was now shining, finally with some welcomed heat. He looked up into the sky, shading his eyes, having lost his hat when he was shot. He felt so exhausted, he staggered as he stumbled, his boots slipping in the fresh mud.

Patch was found not too far away and snickered when he saw Nate approaching him.

"How're you doing, boy?" he asked rhetorically, patting his wet coat, steam rising off as he dried in the sunshine.

Nate stood motionless, leaning on Patch, breathing shallowly, trying to regain his balance. Two sage hens about twenty yards away, brave in the stillness of the day, strutted through the brush. He palmed his Colt by instinct and caught one dead center. He gave a weak smile. *Some instincts won't die,* he thought as Patch carried on grazing, undeterred at the sound of gunfire.

Hobbling to where the bird had fallen, Nate picked up the lifeless fowl. Dizziness and nausea overpowered him as he did so, causing him to rest his hands on his knees to regain his equilibrium. He carried the hen back to the cave, crudely dressing it, then skewered it with a green stick and put it to cook above the red coals of his fire. Patch was now tethered back inside, out of sight in case others came looking for him. He would be in no shape for a fight now, and be easy meat, he knew. The short walk, firing the pistol and back again had drained his strength; sleep would be a blessed relief.

Nate sat gazing into the flames watching the bird spit and drip fat that sizzled and smoked, making his mouth water. He let his mind turn over all the events wondering how things stood in town. He would make one last push to clean it all up and then leave, he decided. He wanted the answers to the questions McKenzie had asked in Denver. Some were clear now, but one or two did not make sense. Once he knew all the answers he could make a definitive move and close it all down. But still some questions nagged at him.

The sage hen was finally cooked and Nate devoured it fervently, relishing the tender meat. Tiredness consuming him once more, he rolled over and slept fitfully.

He was woken by the sound of voices, carrying on the breeze, coming from down below on the lower ledge trail. The fire had burned down to its embers, barely smoldering.

Patch's ears pricked upon hearing the voices and the scrape of metaled hooves on sandstone.

"I tell ya. There is no way he came up here. Why, he was headed north so the boys said. If'n he survived that flood. Jeff don't even know if he did. Probably drowned further down stream. Just because one gun shot gets heard across the whole valley, we're on a damn wild goose chase, I declare. Look, the trail peters out! Unless he grew wings. He surely didn't fly down to the valley below."

The two gun hands stopped and looked ou below them.

"Sure is pretty. You can see why everyone is fightin' over it."

Nate could not see the riders, but guessed they were but thirty yards from his position as he lay low on the rock floor of the cave, screened only by the higher level of his vantage point and the small copse that shielded the cave from view. If they pushed up, he was doomed. He might get one but doubted if he could get both in time. The shooting would draw more men who were doubtless scouring the country for him. In his debilitated state he could not run, he could barely saddle a horse let alone ride it. He steadied his breathing, praying that they would stay on the game trail below.

The swishing of branches could be heard as they moved along getting to where the trail seemed to stop and head into the hazel galleried tunnel. If they found that, they may reason that he had reached the top of the mesa and search harder. The rain had indeed worked for him, washing out all of his tracks. But if they found the hazel route some tracks may still remain. It was then he smelled cigarette smoke and thanked his God, as that would cover any trace of the smell from his fire.

"Yea, I reckon you're right. If'n he's anywhere it'll be with one of them nester families. Jeff reckons he was shot up pretty good and will need care at best if he's still alive. He ain't at the mines or we'd have heard.

"Come on. Let's get back down to the flats and report to the boss that we've covered it. No sign of him or his horse. The other boys may have had more luck."

"Now that's the best thing you've said all day."

The riders turned away, not knowing that Nate was but a few yards away within the copse tucked back in the cave. Pleased that his fire was almost dead and that he'd finished cooking hours before, he let out a slow breath and released the hammer of his cocked Colt.

For two more days he stayed there, setting snares as his strength grew, gathering wild onion, garlic and squaw cabbage. From the stream, he caught two trout and spit roasted them using the fresh herbs.

His strength gradually returned and his wounds had

stopped being red and angry as the signs of infection disappeared. Although his stamina was diminished, Nate knew he would have to be careful to preserve it. The most important thing was his gun speed. With trepidation he strapped on his Colts, tied down the holster and drew. His Navy appeared like magic in his hand. He put in an hour's practice finding that the cavalry twist of his left hand hurt his ribs. He did a border shift, dropped and span, finding that this too hurt and made his wound weep. "Very well. It'll do. Not the best but it will do," he muttered to himself.

Carefully, favoring his left side, he saddled Patch, easing the latigo strap up as tightly as he could, mainly using his right hand. He slipped the reins across the neck and walked to the edge of the trail which was a foot or so higher and almost level with the bottom of the fender. Nate stepped into the stirrup iron, using the verge as a mounting block moving gingerly, trying not to open the wound. He settled as Patch waited patiently for him to sit.

"OK, boy, let's go." They moved off slowly into the dusk following the trail that had originally taken him up to the mesa days ago when he left town to be alone.

Nate hugged all cover afforded by the night and entered from the eastern side of town, coming in by one of the back lanes to arrive at the livery barn. Unbarring the main doors with difficulty, he led Patch through to receive a nicker of recognition and welcome from Buck, who was patiently munching away on a manger of hay. "Hello, boy," he called softly, leading Patch behind him.

"That you, Nate?" a crusty voice called from within the barn as Cal limped out with his bow legged gait. "Well, I'll be. I told 'em that you weren't dead. No body, I says to myself, not dead. Well, you fooled 'em all, they've been a trackin' and scouting every which way for you, boy!" He almost whooped.

"Keep your voice down, you old coot. I don't want 'em to know I'm back. Just keep it quiet for as long as you can. Don't let anyone see Patch."

"Waal, that'll be tough, they come in everyday for their horses and check it over. Sorta half expectin' you, I guess. Say, I know, we'll fix Patch up to look like a black, you'll see. Say, let me help with that," he said seeing Nate struggle with the saddle. "You injured?"

"Yea, got one on the ribs and one across my head. I was lucky, wearing my slicker and it was raining. I suppose I made a poor target. Still didn't do me any good, though. Tell, me, how's Morg?"

"Him and Gorringe are holed up in the jail. They tried to get him one night and the townsfolk came pulled him out of a hole. Got burned a might by a bullet but he's fine. Got sand that boy, I gotta say. But she's waiting to blow soon as they figure you're dead for certain."

"Could you do me a favour?"

"Sure, name it."

"Could you go to Kim's, get her to bring me some food and a clean change of clothes from my room. I'm going to sneak in the back way to the jail. Have you got a cape or a poncho I could wear and an old hat?"

"Sure, I can do that." With which Cal bustled to his office and rooms and returned with an old Mexican style poncho and a beaten up wide brimmed hat. Nate slipped them on pulling the hat down, thanked him and crept off into the darkness not wishing to stay in the livery any longer than necessary. Twice he ducked into alleys on the way as gunmen seemed to be roaming the town expectantly, lawlessness having taken over again.

He banged upon the jail door as loud as he dare. Then finally after a few minutes he was rewarded with a muffled voice.

"Morg? It's me, let me in, quietly," he whispered.

He heard a muffled acknowledgment from within and then bolts being drawn back. He stepped quickly in as soon as the door was opened, motioning with his finger to silence. They would have to pass the cells to get to the front office and rooms. Nate and Morg made it through with barely a glance at the prisoners, Nate stooping keeping his head low. Closing the thick door to the cells, Morg turned and Gorringe rose from his slumbers on the cot, blinking against the lamplight.

"Nate! By the good Lord. We thought you were dead!"

"Keep your voice down! I'd as soon as not let people know I was back. Can I sit down? I'm exhausted and could do with some coffee. Haven't had any for days."

"Sure, sure, sit." And Gorringe bustled, better than he had before, Nate noticed. He still sported a limp, but not needing a crutch any longer. Returning with a steaming mug of sweet coffee, Gorringe placed it before him as Nate slumped onto the cot.

"Now tell us all that happened," Gorringe demanded.

Chapter Twenty-Two

With a good meal inside him and a warm bed, safe in the knowledge that he could relax and be guarded, Nate slept well for twelve hours and woke feeling much better. His head was still sore and his ribs ached. He rose tentatively from the cot and stood, waiting for any dizziness or loss of balance to occur but none came. He would still have to be aware of his limitations of strength and stamina, but he would not be fighting McCrae again.

After washing, he started to clean and oil his guns, reassured by how they felt in his hands and desperate to try his draw again. Once satisfied, he slipped both into their respective holsters, tied down the thong and drew. No direct pain from the ribs, just a constant throb, which he ignored. He slowly attempted a cavalry twist with his left hand, causing his ribs to ignite with pain as he made the awkward move of moving his elbow outwards, rotating from the shoulder. He decided to leave it for a while, knowing that if necessary, he could at least draw the Police Special as back up.

Still, it effectively left just him and Morg to face a load of gunman, if he could persuade him to do so now that he was back. *Is it fair to ask?* he contemplated. It was a stacked deck whichever way he looked at it. He needed a drop or an edge, but what and how to get it.

The front door to the jail opened and he span drawing as he did so, pain erupting from his ribs as he turned.

"Well, you can't be that bad, if you're still trying to shoot people," the newly arrived figure proclaimed. It was Doctor Campbell, closely followed by Morg. The doctor was as severe in his manner as well as his dress of a dark frock coat, string tie and white shirt. Nate liked his brisk, no-nonsense attitude.

"Sit you down and let's take a look at you," he ordered, opening his black bag and removing his stethoscope. "Take your shirt off and we'll see what we've got." Then he began checking Nate over, finally tending to the wound on his head. "Who put this poultice on here?" he asked.

"I did," Nate answered, "used some self-heal I found in the brush."

"Hmm." He grunted and made to peel off the poultice and inspecting it, cleaned the wound. With no more ado he tackled the ribs, rebinding them to aid the movement. When finished he proclaimed, "Well you're better and luckier than you've any right to be. Either of those shots had been an inch or two to the left you'd not be sitting here now.

"I would say rest and take it easy, but I know that is futile advice considering who you are. But that said, if you've come this far under your own steam, you'll make a full recovery. But any dizziness or fainting let me know. I'll come back in two days' time and see how you're doing. In the meantime, try not to get shot or beaten again," he said, sarcasm lining his voice emphasized with a raised eyebrow.

"I'll certainly try, Doc, and thank you again," Nate replied.

He received a snort of disgust in reply and the doctor left being ushered out through the back door by Morg who returned back to the front office.

"Man, you slept so deeply I thought you were dead. Had to check you were still breathing once or twice." Morg laughed. "But now you're back, there are things you need to know. Coffee?"

"Thank you. Go on, I'm listening."

"The marshal and me, we kept things as tight as we could, but it's at night that it gets worse. We moved on some of the gunmen and even closed down two more saloons. But as soon as word got out you were dead; well, it doesn't carry the same weight as it did. I'm not you." Morg shrugged. "A few new gunmen in town, some probably from Jackson's gang showed their faces and are prowling around looking for you. The three you arrested have been arrayed and we have two more we got the drop on in the cells. But the marshal is still sore. I got winged, too, and can't move fast, so we have to go easy and no night patrols. Too much of an easy target."

"OK. I'll get some food. What time is it? I'm famished," Nate responded.

"About one o'clock."

"Can you get me some lunch please, and we'll talk some more."

"Already done and on its way. We get regular meals sent

now as we're short handed. So you just stay put and when Lily comes in from the Square Deal café we'll be dandy."

"Lily, eh?" Nate smiled at Morg. "Well, Montana, you didn't waste any time."

"Ha, nothing happening there," he denied blushing. "Anyway, pays to get on well with those who bring you food."

There was a knock at the door and Nate saw through the crack of a partly open door, a pretty, vivacious girl enter wearing a gingham dress and carrying a tray.

"Morg, you eating for two or something? I couldn't believe when Mama took the order," she teased as he let her in receiving a peck on the cheek.

"N-no, the marshal will be back soon and he eats here as well sometimes," he stammered.

"Why, Morg, honey. Are you blushing 'cause I kissed you? I do declare that is most fetching," she said in an accent that to Nate's ears spoke of the south, possibly Texas.

"Lily, you surely do upset a man's mindset," Morg declared. "But seriously. It could get dangerous. More men are coming into town and I don't want you associated with me or the jail too much."

"I know. They're a bad lot all round. Some tough men amongst 'em. What's going to happen now that the new marshal is dead, or so they say?"

"Don't you fret none, Lily. I think he's still alive, biding his time. Now you'd best go."

"Alright, but don't do anything foolish and call in on your rounds, you hear?" She pecked him on the cheek again sashayed through the door, clearly enjoying his embarrassment.

"Well, hey Morg. She certainly is sparky," Nate teased.

"Now you just hush your mouth. All I need now is Andy to start ribbin' me again and I'll be leavin' real soon."

Nate made a sign for peace, still grinning and proceeded to tuck into the stew, followed by a peach cobbler that he devoured with gusto.

Over coffee and a cigar, Morg explained to Nate the last bit he hadn't previously disclosed. "Of these new men there is one who stands out and frankly, Nate, I don't mind admittin', I wouldn't want to tackle him. Even with the marshal backing me. He came in about a day after you left for Burlington with the gold. He is at the hotel, not troubled anyone, but goes into the Star to play poker most days. He's got that air about him, Nate. He was accused of cheatin' by one of the other gunnies, so I heard, stood up and asked him to apologize or back his play. Well, way the story goes he was faced by two of them; he let them stand, set and they drew first. They didn't have a chance, apparently. No one has seen anyone so fast."

"What's his name and what does he look like?" Nate asked, curious now and pleased that he had returned to his previous speed. He'd faced death before and met his man on equal terms decided by the speed of his draw. Would he finally meet someone faster? Faster even than Sam, of which there had been little if anything to choose between them?

"He's of medium height, slim build, but tough, tanned for a man who spends a lot of time indoors and what I'd say is wolf cautious eyes, as my pappy used to say, mean if he wanted to be. Signed in at the hotel as S. Colt. Oh, and he has two guns like you," Morg finished.

Nate looked hard at him. "Two guns?"

"Yea, just like you. You know, one set for the cross draw, the other at his side."

"Just like me?" Nate asked, his voice almost a whisper.

"Yea, as I said. Why, is it significant? Do you know of him?" Morg asked puzzled.

Nate eased the front legs of the chair to the floor as he had been tilted backwards balancing on just two legs. He removed the cigar from his lips and let a stream of smoke drift into the air, his eyes focused on the middle distance.

"Will he be there now, do you think?"

"Waal, from what I can gather he eats there most days and plays a few hands. Then rides out of town somewhere, I've noticed," Morg finished.

"Right, come with me and bring that shotgun," Nate ordered tying down his holster. Suddenly he felt good, all fear or uncertainty leaving him. If this was his moment, so be it. But he did not think it would be.

He walked out of the jail exposing himself to public debate, regretting that he did not yet have a replacement hat. He slipped the thongs off both his Colts and walked purposefully towards the Northern Star saloon.

"Montana, you stay here. Keep a watchful eye from the doors, but don't come in until I call you. Got it?"

Morg nodded in response.

Then Nate looked carefully over the batwing doors, peering into the dim interior. The saloon was about half full with lunchtime trade, some eating in the dining area, some drinking or playing cards.

"That's him there." Morg nodded at a man dressed in a gambler's cutaway coat, sitting at a table with his back to the wall, studiously looking at his cards. His hat was missing and his brown hair was swept away to reveal the features Morg had so accurately described.

Nate stood for a few moments and then carefully eased himself into the saloon making as little motion as possible. He stood watching the play, then a hubbub of voices started: he had been recognized. Surprise and silence fell, sweeping across the floor. Nate stepped forward towards the table of the gambling gunman. The tension in the saloon was palpable, everyone was shocked to see Nate and to see him actively challenging this new gunman whom everyone thought was hell on wheels. Candy looked on with interest, trying to decide whether to call a halt to the proceedings, telling them to take it outside. But decided that it was now beyond that.

Upon hearing the expectant hush, the gambler looked up from his hand, no expression on his face. "Ah, marshal. I've been expecting you," he said blandly as men quickly cleared from around the table.

Other gunmen watched expectantly, ready to take a stake if they could to shoot Nate in the confusion and gain the reward from their boss. Then they saw Morg slip inside the batwing doors, Colt shotgun at the ready.

"You're under arrest," Nate answered giving him no quarter.

"On what charge?" he asked in the same gentle tone, placing his cards upon the table, pushing back his chair and rising to face Nate, sweeping back the side of his cutaway coat to give access to his guns.

"Being too slow on the draw!" Nate spat, as two hands flew for their Colts.

To those watching no one knew who moved first, or could even claim to see the blur of movement that produced two Colts simultaneously. Everyone waited for the percussion of powder, but it did not come.

"Damn me, boy, if you haven't got quicker!" the gambler said, pinwheeling his Colt and returning it to the leather, a big grin on his face.

"Sam, you old dog. I thought you were dead!" Nate whooped.

"I heard that you were in trouble as usual, getting shot at and like Lazarus decided I'd better come back from the dead and help you out. I do declare, I leave you alone for a few months and I no sooner hear of shootouts, trail gangs, outlaws and then to top it all, you're made a marshal and sheriff. So, I had to come and see for myself."

Nate shook his head a huge smile on his face: "Let me buy you a drink. I could not have wished to see anyone any more than you."

Talk welled up around the saloon, all present pleased that they had not tried to intervene, for it would not have gone well.

As Nate and Sam moved up to the bar, Candy swanned across, her charm on full power.

"Nate, I'm so pleased to see you are alive. We were all worried about you," she purred, placing a warm hand upon his arm. "And aren't you going to introduce me to your mysterious handsome friend?"

"Candy, this is Sam Kennedy. A very good friend of mine and one to whom I owe a great deal."

"Well, Sam. Any friend of Nate's is a friend of mine. These drinks are on the house, boys, from the good bottle Cole," she ordered looking back over her shoulder at the bartender, who nodded an acknowledgement.

"A pleasure to meet you, ma'am, and I'm obliged for the drink," Sam answered smoothly, raising his glass in salutation.

"Ma'am? Candy, please. Would you be the same Sam Kennedy who hails from Brownville Texas?"

"That'll be me, I guess, as I hail from that neck of the woods," he responded noncommittally, yet had a way of making any further enquiry in that regard to be unwelcome. Candy took the hint and moved away to her other customers, flowing charm and flirtation in equal measure.

Morg who had sidled up, could not believe that he was in the company of the famous gunman and ex-ranger. He shook hands with the man and sensing Nate needed to catch up, left with an excuse to watch the jail.

"Sam, I still can't believe it. Man by the name of Brian Wallace, brother to the man I shot on the riverboat, called me out and swore that he had killed you and I was next on his list. Mind, I took exception to that, and he lies in a mighty cold place now."

"So I heard and I thank you for it. Yes, he did shoot me. I was in a card game down to Charlottesville, came up behind, but from a distance so the coward could run away, shot me twice in the back, shouting out that it was for his brother. There was confusion and everyone said, 'You killed Sam Kennedy'. Well, he ran out of the saloon and skedaddled out of town with the sheriff after him. I was carried off to the doc where he removed one slug, but couldn't get to the other one; too close to the spine he said, so there it lay 'til I found one of those fancy Eastern doctors to remove it.

"I put the word out that I was dead as I was so messed up I couldn't defend myself. I paid for a fake funeral, knowin' too many people would be after me if they heard I was still alive and helpless. When I could, I slipped out of town one night, still very weak. The doc got me into a buggy and onto a train north. Then I moved on east up the coast until I found a surgeon. No one had heard of me or knew me by sight.

"Well, this surgeon was good, took me as a sort of challenge. Got the slug out but scared me to death, couldn't raise my legs for days on account of bruisin' to the spinal cord or some such; but gradually it all came back and here I am, good as new. Well almost, but my muscles don't like cold damp weather much." He laughed before continuing.

"Then I set myself on a trail of vengeance to get the man who did it. By the time I was up and about and headed west again, I heard the news that you shot Wallace. Seems like you're getting a reputation, Nate. You'll have to go easy, it can change a man, I know."

"I know only too well. I'm trying to set myself up as a cattleman and play down the gunfighting."

"Mmm, same as Clay Alison, but he does like to hooray the town at the end of the drive and get himself into trouble with his brothers. Mind, he has been pushed into it followin' the war just like you and many another southern boy.

"Heard about your breaking the herd cutters and facing down Old Man Randall to save a farmer's life, that was well done. Now you're a trail boss helping the underdog, isn't that what all you English do, anyway?" He smiled.

"It is, and you seem to know a lot."

"News travels on the range telegraph, you know that. Then I thought to catch up with you in Dodge, but Charlie Basset said you'd moved on again after sorting those herd cutters at the pens. Then news came of a range war up here, where they were hiring guns and sure enough, a man called Nate Carlton was mixed up in it. I couldn't believe you were dead, so I hung around waiting to see who was what and where, and it sure is confusin'. So how about you tell me all about it over a decent cup of coffee?"

Nate agreed and they left for the Square Deal café.

As soon as they were gone, Candy left for her rooms, changing into more conservative street clothes and left by the back door and headed for the bank. She looked along the street to ensure that Nate and Sam were out of sight and entered the bank asking for Moises Letterman.

Once inside, with the door closed, Moises offered her a seat sensing all was not well. "You need to be careful coming here in the middle of the day, Candy." he warned.

"Oh, do I? Well, we have more to worry about than that. Nate Carlton is back from the dead and that new gambler who came into town a few days ago? Well turns out he is not only a friend of the marshal, but is the famous gunman from Brownsville, Sam Kennedy. He is also an ex-ranger. I saw them draw, Moises, they're both so fast, I've never seen anything like it.

"Things are getting out of hand: first the ore gets through; then the nesters are unified, the sweet land deal we had going is proving not so easy. Hart's getting cold feet and now Carlton turns up alive and reinforced with one of the most deadly gunfighters in the west.

"He's also closed down most of the bad elements in town." Her voice rose in anger. "The gunmen we've hired need paying and are getting restless or worried and drifting away. Jackson lost a lot of men both in the Wells Fargo raid and on the trail to Burlington. Word is getting out, we need to resolve this soon!" she ranted, no longer looking the ravishing saloon owner but with her face twisted in hate and anger.

"So, he's alive, is he? Well, he must be dealt with, either with or without this man Kennedy. He is after all just one man and everyone has their price."

"You haven't seen them together. There is a bond between them, more than just money could break and both are so damn moral. Believe me, I know. I serve men all day long and know every kind there is and what makes them tick. These two are different. I may be a woman but Carlton is sweet on that Hart girl from what I can tell or I'd have got to him before. She is the reason he was here in the first place. If not for him it would all be clear and settled now. The town would be ours and the railroad coming our way with the mines to pay for everything. That stupid cow eyed bitch leading him on," she cursed.

"Why not use it for us?" Letterman asked, his mind

working all angles on the problem. "Use her as bait? Lure him out and kill him, or get her on side and change his mind."

"Might have worked in the beginning if we'd known what we were up against but not now, it's too late and I doubt he'll leave town now, having laid for him once and missed," she replied scornfully.

"Look here. He can't close us down for no reason. It has to be against the law. We're all respectable citizens. I run a bank, you run a clean saloon who breaks no laws and Hart brings money in through cattle and trade. Why, that old biddy of his is on more town and church committees than a congressman running for office.

"Oh, he can grumble and complain. He might even put a wanted poster out on Jackson, but so what? What can he do? We have the law on our side and the townsfolk won't want our business out. If he causes gun trouble, why we'll call in the U.S. Marshal and get him on side and soon my nephew will have the contract set up for the railroad.

"As soon as he puts a foot wrong, we'll have him," he carried on assuredly.

"I hope that you're right. I have a bad feeling about all this, it's not going to plan." She brooked no rebuttal of this, turned and left without waiting to hear his reply.

Returning to her saloon Candy sent a message out to Jackson at his hideout asking him to come to town. A similar message was sent to Charles Hart at the Circle.

Chapter Twenty-Three

"So you say that it is Hart, Letterman and Jackson that are all in this together from what you can tell?"

"Yes, and as much as I hate to say this, Candy as well. They are also all spread out. How do you take one without the other and we haven't the guns or manpower to raid the Jackson hideout. We don't know how many we'd be facing. Hart has all intents and purposes done nothing wrong, other than employing some rather shady hands, who use guns better than a rope. The bad element has gone but the roots of it all are still here. That's what we have to dig out and stop once and for all. They still have power, land and money, and control half the businesses in town."

Sam thought for a moment. "We had a similar situation with a border town not so long ago, bad elements took over and it all balanced on ownership, all to do with old Mexican Land Grants. Hey, though maybe that's it. You say McKenzie bought some railroad stock when he was in Denver?"

"We both did, he bought some for me, too. He has hopefully written to them asking for full disclosure as a shareholder and explaining that there are some underhand dealings going on; people being driven from their homes etc. He also asked if Letterman was involved or Hart. He seems to know a few people back east which was helpful. I also got Yates to file a claim on the workings that have been carried out on his land. So all that strip on this side of the arroyo is now registered as a claim, both with him and the mining company."

"Good. Now we simply cut off the hydra's head." Sam smiled. "Yes, I have some book learning too, you know."

"I never doubted it for a moment. Well first we send some telegrams, so we need to take over the telegraph office on official business. Then once we have those answers, we make our play. But first we need to organize a secret town council meeting, not including Letterman or Candy. Can you do that?"

"Of course, then let's get going." He rose, paid for the coffee and the two men made for the telegraph office.

Once there they ordered the clerk to leave: "What do you mean leave, marshal? This is my place of work. I'm here as an official of the company," he stated indignantly as he was bustled out of the door.

"I'm sure you are and mister Letterman would love to know what we are doing and who we are sending telegrams to, but on this occasion, he is not going to, now get out!" Nate shouted. "We'll pay for the service but I don't want you or anyone else knowing my business."

The clerk scuttled out in an irate manner and stormed off to Moises Letterman's bank.

"Right, let's get moving before that nice mister Letterman turns up," Sam said as he locked the door and Nate got busy with the key.

Ten minutes later Letterman appeared with the clerk, banging upon the locked door.

Sam just smiled at them and ignored the noise.

"Let me in, I demand to be let in," Letterman called.

"Locks jammed, sir. We'll have it open soon. Don't you worry," Sam responded charmingly. Half an hour later Nate had all he wanted in terms of answers and he placed a few dollars on the counter and unlocked the door. He let the clerk and Letterman in, much to the amusement of the crowd who had gathered in front to see what all the noise was about.

"What is the meaning of this?" Letterman demanded pompously. "I'll have you removed from office, marshal. I shall summon the town council and have you removed!" he stormed. By which time it was too late. Nate didn't even bother to explain, just told the clerk that the money for the telegrams was on the counter. He and Sam walked away with threats ringing loud in their ears heeding nothing.

"Now for the next part. Hopefully Morg will have rounded up all the town councilors whilst we had Letterman distracted," Nate muttered quietly.

They walked on past the jail to one of the side streets and knocked upon the door of Marshal Gorringe's house. The parlor was full with Gorringe, Doctor. Campbell and six other men already present; including Judge Raybold and

Mayor Roberts. Nate gratefully accepted a cup of coffee and sat down to wait for the final two members of the council to arrive, followed by McKenzie who had been summoned from the mines.

When they did, he stood and called for silence.

"Thank you, gentlemen, for humoring me and coming at such short notice. There are a number of things that you need to know. But first let me say that we are nearly there. Soon I can confidentially say that you will be free from the noose of evil that has held your town in a stranglehold. You have given me free rein and I hope I haven't disappointed even if you may, at times, have disputed my methods.

"Now I have here the means to finally free you and the town from all the killings and disruption. But it must be done legally and this rests with you. It's ultimately your decision and on your head be it if you turn me down. Because Sam, who I've now sworn in as a deputy and Morg, will walk and leave you to resolve it yourselves."

Nate paused letting the words sink in. A few looked at each other doubt written across their faces, nervous when faced with such an ultimatum.

"This is what I propose." With which Nate outlined his plan backed by the information he had received via the telegrams.

It was an hour later that he left the meeting, feeling more drained than when he had faced a gun battle. The councilors had argued and disputed his findings, surprised and dismayed at how they had been duped and what they needed to pass to make his next actions legal and binding. Finally, they had all agreed with two abstentions, but had the necessary votes to make the mandates binding and legal. He now had the authority for his next actions.

Nate left the meeting accompanied by Sam and bumped into Morg hurrying to meet them.

"Hart's in town and his daughter, Nate. She's been asking for you. And, Jackson's horse is in the corral behind the Northern Star. They're all gathering."

"Thanks ,Morg. Where's Isobel?"

"At the marshal's office waiting for you."

Nate nodded and walked off purposefully, not looking forward to his next meeting with Isobel. He took a deep breath and entered the office.

Isobel eased her pacing of the floor, spinning in the moment to face him.

Nate saw a lovely woman, her copper hair highlighted and burnished by the sun, a tanned face with a Stetson hanging by the storm strap at her throat. She wore an ivory shirtwaist complimenting her complexion, holding leather riding gloves in her hand which she slapped down upon her thigh.

"Nate! Where have you been? They said you were dead! I was so worried when you didn't make our date. I heard about the hold ups and raids upon Wells Fargo. When will this all end?"

"Isobel, please let me explain," Nate began and set about his explanation of events that led to the gold and silver ore being transported, thwarting the outlaws and the dry gulching he suffered at the hands of the two outlaws. She listened in silence, her face a mixture of emotions as he proceeded with his tale.

Isobel then took a deep breath, clearly exasperated. "More deaths, Nate. More men killed! Will this ever end? And still you put all your faith in your guns," she fumed.

"It is all I have, for there is no law in the west save that brought by the gun and the just men who wield them. Do you believe that an unarmed man wearing just a badge would survive many minutes? No, the only law west of the Ohio is enforced by the gun and the fear of the man who wields it in the name of righteousness with the law on his side.

"If you cannot see that, then you are blind to good and evil, right and wrong."

"Right and wrong?" she snapped, color rising in her cheeks. "You are as bad as the men you kill and you know? I think that you enjoy it. You enjoy the power of the gun you use."

"What? You truly believe that? You come out here with your eastern ideas, where if there is a problem you call a policeman on a street corner. You want law and order, but you won't pay the price or heed the cost," he responded exasperatedly.

They both stood, Isobel with her hands clenched by her side in anger stamping her foot in frustration. "You, you... No more gunfights, Nate, or what we have is finished. Put up your guns, show me you mean it, that you care about peace and no violence."

"That is your final word?"

"Yes."

"Then look to your father, for he is as bad as any. He is behind this as much as anyone. Ask him about guns and the law," he shouted back losing his temper.

Isobel stamped her foot once more, with a face drawn in lines of hurt and anger. She fled the office, crying tears of pain as she went.

Sam and Morg entered the office shortly after, looking slightly shame faced; sound carried and they heard most of what was said.

Morg offered gravely: "Sorry, Nate, we heard a bit of it. She'll come round I'm sure. She's eastern it'll just take time."

"No, sadly I don't think she will, Morg," he said softly.

Minutes later papers were delivered, signed by all the members of the council who were present at the meeting, confirming the new ordinances that Nate had proposed.

"These..." Nate waved the papers in his hand. "...along with the enquiries McKenzie made at Denver from his lawyer there, are enough to get the job done."

"Now what?" Sam asked.

"We give it another half an hour then all the pigeons will be home to roost and we can gather them all together. I saw some of Hart's gun hands in town, too, so they will be there. You sure you're up for this, Sam? Even with the townsmen backing us, it's going to be rather tense."

Sam laughed. "You English certainly have a way with the art of under statement! Tense you say? It will be downright bloody dangerous and I wouldn't miss it for the world. We'll go loaded for bear and those who we can't dissuade, we'll cut loose."

Morg entered the jail a while later. "All the posters are up around town offerin' the reward for Stu Jackson," he said, dropping the hammer and tacks upon the desk with a smile.

"Oh, and Letterman is in there and guess who else? McCrae and Tye Lewis!"

"McCrae!" Nate exclaimed. "Well, well. All together for the showdown."

The door opened again and in marched the judge and a couple of stout-hearted townsmen, all with shotguns and rifles.

"Good evening, gentlemen. I'm glad that you could make it to the party." Nate greeted them grimly. They all had long guns and pistols at their hips, the judge as ever with his shotgun carried balanced under his arm.

"Now, remember I don't want any of you in the line of fire. You stay at the back entrance, to mop up any who try to get out. I will warn them you're waiting so they don't charge out. You just shout when you're in position, so they know I'm not bluffing and that I have backing for all of this."

They all nodded and Gorringe limped in.

"Andy, what are you doing here?"

"It's my town. I'm goin' to help with all this. I won't be no good for fancy gunplay, but I can back up from the street with my rifle from cover." With which he raised his Winchester in his left hand and patted his pistol with his right.

"Well then, we're all set," Nate said and picked up a spare Remington Beals revolver from the desk, gave the loads a final check and shoved it in his belt at his back. He noticed Sam's raised eyebrow. "Picked it up from the gunsmith, still having trouble from the ribs with the cavalry twist, so may need another gun fast and this, as you know, won't go off by mistake. The new safety milling of the chamber makes it safe. Feels a lot like my Navy, too."

"Only five shots, but a good choice for a back-up," Sam applauded.

"If I'm still standing. I would hope to have got the job done." Nate gave a wry smile. He tied down his holster, slipped the two thongs from his Colts, stood and said: "Shall we go, gentlemen?"

There were nods all round and as the townsmen left through the back door, Nate, Sam, Morg and Gorringe marched down the main street. Eyes were wary, looking up and out as they passed the buildings. Gorringe, his Winchester at the ready, saw a flash of light from a balcony above the Northern Star. He shouldered his rifle and fired, giving no quarter. There was a cry; and a sickening thud as the would be gunman fell over the rail to drop to the ground below.

The others had guns either drawn or raising. "Nice shot, Andy," Nate said calmly rebolstering his Colt as he saw it was the gun hand Chas Goodman who had waylaid him out at the shooting range.

"My pleasure," he offered. "One less to worry about."

They paused at the batwing doors, all silent within after the shot.

Gorringe stood at the window, rifle ready at a signal from Nate who stepped inside followed by Sam and Morg with both men fanning out on either side of him.

"Good evening, gentlemen," he said into the silence, suddenly calm within himself, knowing all along that it would come to this as soon a she had donned the badge, seemingly an age. His adrenaline had spiked along the street, but as soon as he walked through the saloon door, he became focused, everything viewed with clarity. It helped having Sam at his side, there was no man with whom he would rather face these odds.

The saloon was filled with the usual girls employed by Candy. They all looked nervous. A mixture of cowhands and gunmen sat at tables or lined the bar, each looking on with interest.

Letterman was at the bar, a whiskey in his hand, by his side stood Hart.

At a table nearby was Stu Jackson, looking calm and mean. His eyes were bloodshot with a nervous energy about him.

There was no sign of Candy. Then his eyes roved upwards. She was standing on the balcony above, leaning provocatively on the rail, a gunman by her side. *Too close*, Nate thought intuitively.

Then he spotted McCrae at a table by the stairs, still yellow with bruises on his face and a pistol on the table before him. Two more men sat at his side, evil looking, one with a shotgun.

Others were visible who had been caught in the pass by the dynamite, Nate noticed and gun hands from Hart's ranch. He saw that Hart was sweating in fear. This was not his play, he was an easterner, forced by his actions to be part of this final showdown. A man who had manufactured and supplied armaments and munitions to soldiers on the northern ranks, not one who stood in the line of fire. Now he was faced with the stark reality of conflict and didn't like it one bit.

"Evening, marshal," Candy called from the balcony. "What can I do for you?"

It was a good ploy to distract him and maybe the others, draw their eyeline away from the crowds below. But Sam had taught him well. He answered her by not looking up, knowing that any distraction would set it off and be his last action. Nate pulled his own ace in the hole, ignoring Candy's question. Everyone watched, ready for any sign of weakness. They knew what they faced: two of the fastest gunfighters they had ever seen blessed with blinding speed. No one wanted to die first.

"You all set back there, judge, mayor?" he shouted.

They thought it was a bluff until they heard the response. "Sure are, marshal. We're all ready for them, shotguns and rifles at the ready. Send 'em out those who want to leave peaceable, but they'd better be unarmed, or we shoot on sight."

There were gasps and nervous looks all around especially from the cowhands. They were loyal to their brand but wanted no part of this.

"Andy, you there?" Nate shouted, all the time watching everyone's movement.

A crash of glass was heard from the front window and then another which surprised Nate.

It was Jim, the Wells Fargo guard at the other window. "Got 'em covered, Nate, "just say the word," he said confidently. And suddenly to those present it was not so easy, the odds were still in their favour, but now extra men were mostly hidden from view, well armed and ready.

Letterman began his pompous response. "Marshal, you can't do this! You have no authority breaking in here, damaging property to suit your own ideas of law and order. This is a peaceful gathering in a legal saloon. It is also not on the list of places that you posted to be closed."

There were nods from around the room as others took up the cries, including Charles Hart, who nodded like a yoyo.

Nate cut across before all was lost, silencing them: "Nice try, Letterman. Let me just fill you in. There are two new city ordinances that have just been passed by the council. You were absent, but not needed. So let me be brief. All premises harboring criminals or men wanted by the law can be closed. Anyone associated with those said premises, or guilty of harboring aiding or abetting those criminals is just as guilty and can be charged. Including..." Here, Nate paused for affect. "...including you, Letterman. You own the Northern Star, far more than miss Candy, up there. Jackson is a wanted man, so are others here, wanted in connection with the attempted stage robbery and ore raid. There are dodgers posted around town. That means you're all guilty."

There were rumbles of surprise here at this disclosure, before he continued. "I know all about your plans for the railroad and what your nephew has been up to in the east. It's not going to happen. We've bought stock. It's done, finished, you're all here illegally. Yates has filed on the mine workings on his land, and you, gunnies, you won't get paid; they've got no more money. Letterman and Hart will welch on you, the whole thing is gone to hell and back. You ride now, you get out with your hides.

"Anyone who wants out now's your chance, unbuckle and leave. Out the back way and keep out of the line of fire."

It started like a trickle as gun belts from the cowhands dropped, especially at the back of the saloon, as they headed for the door. Some were out in a flash, others went for front doors as quick as they could around the sides of the line of fire. It didn't last.

"Letterman, Hart, Jackson, McCrae. You all are under arrest," Nate said clearly.

The remaining saloon girls ran for the stairs and under this cover, Jackson stood up: "To hell with you, marshal. They say you're fast. How good are you without the back up of your paid killer?" He didn't wait for an answer. As he stood he raised his right hand drawing his Smith & Wesson in a smooth fast action.

Nate caught the flicker of movement, drawing by instinct, hand a blur, loosing two shots as Jackson stood in amazement seeing the red stain spread across his chest. He continued to try to raise the pistol, still uncomprehending of how he had been beaten. Nate fired a third shot as soon as he thought the danger was still present. The bullet entered Jackson's head throwing him backwards.

Then all hell broke loose. Two of the men at Jackson's table tipped it over, throwing up the wooden circle as cover. Nate caught one in the turn and the other threw down on him with a snap shot at the pall of powder smoke surrounding him, missing in his haste. Nate steadied himself, pulled the trigger once and shot him through the exposed shoulder as the bullet caught the edge of the table sending splinters into his eyes. He screamed in agony falling backwards.

Sam had drawn at the same time catching two gunmen who took the cards in the opportunity, both fell dead, thrown backwards, chest shot. Cowhands and saloon girls had dropped to the floor.

McCrae had grabbed the pistol on the table seizing the opportunity of distraction. Nate altered his aim slightly, crouching, presenting a smaller target, pumping two shots into his bulky frame, one taking him in the throat with an arc of arterial blood.

A rifle cracked from the window, once, twice, as fast as Jim Oates could work the lever and the two barman from the Barrel saloon fell dead, impossible for Jim to miss at that range with a Winchester.

Letterman had pulled a pistol from a concealed shoulder holster, with surprising dexterity; Sam saw the move and let fly, two bullets ruining his fancy silk vest. He collapsed grasping the bar for support.

As the barman brought up a sawn off shotgun, Morg pulled the trigger on his own, blowing him nearly in half with the charge at such short range. Part of the spread of deadly steel pellets caught Hart in the shoulder, spinning him around and he mewled in pain. He sagged to the floor to lie in a pool of blood beside the gruesome body of Letterman.

Two more gunmen dropped to Gorringe's rifle, one of whom was his traitorous ex-deputy, Tye Lewis, who now stared sightless at the ceiling. Black powder smoke hung in drifts, stifling the air with a sulphureous smell mixing with the sickly metallic, sweet smell of blood and gore.

Gunmen further back had sought cover behind tables, that proved useless as Jim and Gorringe beat a tattoo of lead across the inadequate cover, splintering it, causing them to rise up and be cut down by Nate and Sam.

Then it stopped as suddenly as it started. Cries of the wounded filled the air: two saloon girls and cowhands had been hit in the cross fire.

"Your boss is dead, give it up," Nate shouted into the misting swirls of powder.

"You're surrounded behind, too," came Judge Raybold's shout from the rear.

Guns were dropped or thrown forward as men rose, hands raised with cries for surrender.

Nate rose from his crouch looking now upwards to see Candy gone and two men pointing six guns down at him and Sam from the landing above. "Sam!" Nate shouted in warning. He delivered a border shift, grabbing the Beales from his back, firing as soon as he lined on them.

No one could say who killed the two gunmen, ten bullets were lodged in their bodies. Anyone would have killed them as Sam, Nate, Jim and Andy Gorringe all let rip simultaneously. The gunmen jerked and spasmed, shot to doll rags as they fell.

The silence following the action was deafening. Everyone stood as though transfixed. A bottle rolled and crashed to the floor. Nate and Sam reacted by lining ready to fire at the perceived threat, each on a hair trigger.

Nate gave a taut laugh sounding strained in the silence,

everyone holding their breath waiting for the crash of powder to follow.

Sam laughed. "Now what did that poor lil ol' bottle do to us?" he asked.

Nate shook his head in disgust. "OK, all you boys drop your belts. Come ahead, Judge, all clear but be wary. Any sign of trouble shoot and ask questions later," he advised.

It put all present on notice not to try anything stupid. Doctor Campbell arrived at the doors of the saloon. "If you've finished shooting everyone now, can I come and mend what you've broken?" he asked sourly, pushing through the doors.

"Doctor see to me," Hart cried.

With barely a glance, Campbell looked over and then ignored him, instead going to the two wounded saloon girls as they lay sobbing at the bottom of the stairs. One had been burned by a bullet across her back, but the other girl was more seriously wounded and losing blood rapidly.

He opened his bag with a look of concern upon his face. "Andy, go and fetch Nurse Mallory, I shall need help," he shouted.

Andy Gorringe limped off in search of the nurse.

Nate also shouted for him to bring back Sheila Winn. As he turned he saw blood dripping down onto the floor beneath Sam's feet. Sam had no recollection of being hit, knowing that sometimes it was like that in the heat of the moment. If it didn't stop you, you didn't know it. "Nah, nothing but a scratch," Sam said cupping his hand to his shirt as it came off red and sticky.

"Sam, sit down, that's an order. Doc, when you're

ready," Nate asked. At which both Nurse Mallory and Sheila Winn entered the saloon followed by her husband. She had a rifle in her hand and a basket of bandages in the other.

"Didn't know which to bring," she said blithely.

Nate propositioned her to follow him upstairs. "I need a lady with me. Candy is up there and I want a female and a witness. I've never shot a woman and have no intention of doing so."

The wounded saloon girl, called out: "Marshal, I'll gladly go. That bitch sold us out and may have killed Sue. I'll shoot her myself if you give me a gun!"

"No need, but another pair of eyes won't hurt," Nate answered surprised at her vehemence.

They returned minutes later empty handed to questioning looks. "She has run away. Went out of the window, slid down sheets and her bag is gone. The safe door is open. I'm glad in a way, I would hate to have shot her," Nate said.

He then looked to Sam who was being tended by the doctor, the saloon girl being carried upstairs to a bed swathed in bandages, looking deathly pale.

Chapter Twenty-Four

The following evening, Sam was in bed at the hotel, strapped up and the bullet removed. Nate was at his side in his room leaning back on a chair, balancing on two legs. Oil lamps lit the room and a supper tray with a half-finished meal lying on top of Sam's bed to one side. His appetite not being what it was.

They had cleaned up the saloon and all the bad element had left town. Some were now lodged at the jail especially those who had been in Jackson's gang and on the raid of the mining ore. For the first time in as long as anyone could remember there had been no shootings, gunplay or knife fights that night. All was quiet and peaceful.

The saloon had been the last straw and with Letterman and Jackson dead; Hart wounded and Candy gone, the violence had dwindled. The town had won its battle for law and order.

There was a knock at the door.

"Come in," Sam called out, stopping his conversation with Nate.

The door opened to reveal Isobel Hart.

Nate let the chair fall forward and stood: "Isobel," he said.

"Surprised? Well, I don't see why you should be. You two shot my father and left him lying in a pool of blood!" she began, giving no pause for niceties.

"Isobel, we didn't shoot him," Nate replied.

"No, well you may as well have. Guns, it's always down to guns. You burst in there arresting Letterman, a respectable banker my father tells me, and all hell broke loose. More men killed and that poor saloon girl. All for what? To say that you won? The great Nate Carlton gunfighter extraordinaire, saves the town. And your friend here is just as bad. My father may lose his arm all because you had to go in shooting regardless of innocent by-standers.

"Whether you pulled the trigger or not, you may as well have. Well, I hope that you are both satisfied. You will both recover and live to ride off and shoot up another town somewhere. I never want to see you again, Nate. We are leaving for the east once my father recovers. And good riddance to this damned awful country!" She turned on her heel slamming the door.

Nate and Sam looked at each other stunned. "Well, I think that settles that," Nate said calmly. "She's worse than a blue norther."

"She is and will never settle out here. Her father has clearly spun his side of the tale and she'll never hear anything against him. Are you going to arrest him?"

"That's not up to me, thankfully. All the evidence is there, as much as it is and now it's for Judge Raybold to decide what is to be done. Most of the truly bad men are dead. I believe he was being pressured and blackmailed. Maybe for some shabby dealings in munitions? Underhand dealings? Who knows. It will be difficult to prove much, other than by association. He may have been behind pushing the nesters out and the raid on Yates's, but it was never his hand on the trigger. Maybe he's suffered enough. Either way, I don't care. I'm finished. I will resign tomorrow. Gorringe is back and he's welcome to it."

There was then another knock on the door.

"Who is it?" Sam asked, more cautious now.

"It's Isobel," came an emotional voice patently upset. "Can I come in? I want to apologize. I realise how rude I was and I'm so sorry."

Nate and Sam looked at each other surprised.

Sam raised his eyebrows questioningly, Nate nodded in agreement at which Sam said, "Sure, come ahead."

The door nob turned as she said thanks, and she was pushed inwards quickly, behind her was a woman in a maid's uniform: hair hidden under a cap, thick spectacles on her nose and holding a Remington Rimfire Derringer that was pushed into Isobel's head just behind the ear.

"Get inside, you stupid girl!" the maid shouted, kicking back the door with her heel. "You two sit fast or I blow her brains out. This is a Remington four shot so I've enough for both of you. As fast as you are, Nate. You'll not beat me to blow her head off."

"Candy!" Nate said, taking a while to recognise the transformed mousy looking maid before him.

"Well clever you, marshal, just a little too late. Hold still, missy," she said taking a tighter grip into the thick locks of Isobel's hair, pulling her head back as tears slid down her face, eyes wide with fear, sniffing through the pain. "Though I've got to thank you for finding this pair and getting me in here."

Nate looked on aghast wondering how he had ever thought Candy was attractive, her features now twisted and distorted in hate, eyes a brittle blue and unforgiving.

"What do you want, Candy? Leave the girl alone, she's not part of this. Shoot me if you wish."

"Ever the chivalrous gentlemen, huh, Nate?" She sneered. "Well, it's too late. You ruined all my plans, all the money gone, Letterman dead; no recourse to what's mine; everything sunk into that saloon and now I'm on the run with little to my name. And it's all your fault. You and that gunslinging friend of yours. Why couldn't you just leave or take up with this doe eyed little cow and be gone.

"Oh no, you had to take a hand in the game all because some deputy got shot. So what. But your honor and her stupid father did this. Yes, girly, I heard your rant. Well, your pappy's as guilty as the rest of us in his own way. Land hungry, greedy. Who do you think called the raid on those settlers? Yes, your pompous old man. Easy, Nate, keep your hands away from those guns," she snapped as he had been inching closer to get an advantage. "Well, now your hatred of guns is going to get worse because I'm going shoot your beau in front of your eyes.

"Now lift them out carefully, finger and thumb butts forward." Nate started to comply. "Just one twitch and I'll pull this trigger, I warn you," she continued.

Sam watched Nate's progress, both seeming to read the other, looking for an edge. With all eyes on Nate, Sam had inched his hand across the covers to be on the tray edge, and hoped Nate had noticed.

One thing Sam had taught Nate was reaction time. No matter how primed a person, if the unexpected happened it distracted and took a fraction of a second for the brain to get back on track and send messages. Nate now held both revolvers butts towards Candy.

"Good boy," she purred sarcastically.

The tray flew upwards, flipping, sending glass, plates, cutlery and a cup crashing to the floor. Candy was taken by surprise thinking Sam was out of the game as his gun hung in its holster on the bed post behind him. In doing so, to see, she moved her and Isobel to the left exposing herself even more to Nate. He did the fastest Road Agent's Spin of his life, the Colts pinwheeling on his fingers with a life of their own. As she looked back the last thing she saw were two flashes of orange flame as the guns roared. She was flung back, her head showing two blue holes at the front, the back a gory mess. The Remington discharged into the wall, missing Isobel's head by a fraction of an inch. She let out a piecing scream, ranting and wailing hysterically.

Nate ran forward kicking Candy's gun from her hand feeling physically sick. He had killed a woman.

Three days' later Nate's horses were saddled in front of the jail house. Already mounted was Morg who had decided to go and work for him in Texas and he hoped Lily would follow.

Sheriff Gorringe was there leaning on the rail post. "Nate, whatever the others think or say, I'm grateful. We'd have lost everything without you. You sacrificed a lot and I'll always know that." He offered a calloused palm to Nate who shook his hand vigorously.

"Oh, I nearly forgot," he muttered and turned to his office, coming back out onto the sidewalk with a black Stetson in his hand. It had silver conchos in a decorative band around the lower crown. "Isobel said to say that there is a note in the crown, but not to read it until you are on the trail."

Nate was surprised, taking the hat and placing it upon his head, forcing it to the correct shape and the jack deuce angle. He nodded saying nothing and went to mount Buck, picking up the lead reins of Patch.

A slouched figure rode up, riding a big black horse: "Sam, what the hell?"

"Got to ride, this place will kill me," he said.

Nate shook his head in disbelief. "You ready, Montana? Then let's ride."

He swung up into the saddle and never looked back upon the town that had made him a lawman and rode out along the street heading south.

Afterword

A message from Simon:

I know that you have a million choices of books to read and I can't tell you how much it means to me that you chose time to read one of my books. I really hope that you enjoyed it and found it entertaining.

If you did I would appreciate a few more minutes of your time, if I may humbly ask you to leave a review for other readers who may be trying to select their next reading material.

If for any reason you were not satisfied with this book please do let me know by emailing me at simon@ simonfairfaxauthor.com

The satisfaction of my readers and feedback are important to me.

About the Author

ABOUT THE AUTHOR

Simon Fairfax writes in two different genres: International financial thrillers and medieval fiction.

He is a former Chartered Surveyor, Editor of an online polo magazine (having played polo for a number of years) and has practiced martial arts, fencing and shooting. He now restores old classic sports cars for fun.

As a lover of crime thrillers and espionage, Simon turned what is seen by others as a dull 9 – 5 job into something that is exciting, and as close to real life as possible, with Rupert Brett, his unwilling hero.

His latest medieval series now has three books released in a proposed 6 book series. The first, A Knight and a Spy 1410, is set in a tumultuous time at the English court. It tells the story of Jamie de Grispere, squire in training and his two companions as they fight the French to save Calais, Welsh treason and Scottish revolts. The fourth in the series, A Knight and a Spy 1413 will be published on the 31st August 2022.

Details of all his books can be found at www.simonfairfax.com or email him at simonfairfaxauthor@gmail.com

Made in United States
Troutdale, OR
08/16/2024

22062317R00146